Divine
ROYALTY

Shelli Humphrey

Dedication

This book is dedicated to my sister who was my inspiration behind Catalina. The bond between Catalina and Anastasia mirrors that of mine and my sister's, for that despite the distance between us we are still connected by heart and soul.

I also dedicate this book to my niece Anastasia, who's name I borrowed for my main character. From the first time I met my little niece, I sensed a strong but wild spirit. When I was thinking of a name for my main character, I knew I needed one that embodied the strength and ferocity that the character was filled with. Every time I tried a name, it felt wrong and my niece's face kept popping into my head. Finally, something felt right, and thus Queen Anastasia was born.

Chapter One

Looking up at the full moon, I was surprised to see there was a purple haze covering it. Thinking back to my studies of the moon, I realized what it meant. There was no time to waste. I headed inside to find my spell book and the box of herbs I had been saving for this day.

Heading out to my garden, I set up the circle, and got started putting the herbs together for the spell. Once the fire was built and the herbs were ready, I centered myself and cast the circle. As the elements came alive, I started the incantation.

> *Et luna sub regium*
> *Et interpellabit majores natu*
> *et aperuerit ostium*
> *et enutries me*

After repeating the incantation thrice, I felt the power of my words flow through me. Above the flames of my fire, a purple portal opened and through it I could see the silhouette of a large castle. As I stepped closer and got ready to walk through the portal, a hand reached out and grabbed hold of me, pulling me through.

As the vertigo passed, she came into view. Catalina stood in front of me with all of her beauty and power. All of a sudden, I was engulfed in her presence, as she threw her arms around me. "I cannot believe you are finally home! I have been waiting so long for this day." She exclaimed with happiness. "Lina how I have missed you!" I cried as I hugged my sister back, "But how did you know?" She looked at me like I was a young child asking an obvious question. "When the sun rose this morning, it was not normal. Look." She told me as she pointed behind me. I turned to see the sun shining bright but all the rays coming off of it were purple. "As soon as I saw that, I saddled up my horse and rode out here. I have been sitting here waiting for the portal all day. It is just about dinner time. Oh how our parents will be so surprised. Oo and Michael too." She said, her words filled with excitement, "Come now. We must hurry, if we are to get back before dessert."

We jumped on her horse and rode back to the castle as fast as her beautiful mare could move. The guards at the gates were stunned to see me with my sister, as were the servants we passed in the halls. Outside the banquet hall I stopped. "What do I say? It has been so long!" I cried to her, the realization that I was finally home just sinking in now. "Do not worry. You probably will not have to talk much if I know our parents and you know Michael will not make you say anything if you do not want to." She said as she stepped forward to open the doors. I hid behind her, as she walked up to our parents table, and waited for her to signal me.

"Where have you been Catalina? You almost missed

dinner." Our mother's voice rang in my ears like the most beautiful sound in the world.

"I am sorry Mother. I was out picking something up that we thought lost forever." Catalina said mysteriously.

"What do you mean?" Mother asked confused. At Mother's question, I stepped out from behind my sister.

The entire room went silent except for my mother who cried out as she jumped from her seat and ran to me. She threw her arms around me, as the tears started falling from her eyes.

"My sweet sweet girl, how I have missed you! Oh Goddess thank you for bringing her home!" My mother whispered in my ear as I wrapped my arms around her.

I looked up from her shoulder to see Michael standing a few feet behind her. As Mother released me and stepped away, he ran up to me and kissed me. I melted into his arms. I had never felt right in that other realm. I always felt as if a piece of me was missing, and here it was. As my betrothed released my lips, I smiled up at him with tears in my eyes.

"You are home now my love." He said sweetly as he wiped away a tear that managed to escape down my cheek.

As we all sat down and a servant brought Catalina and I some food, my father leaned over and kissed my cheek before turning to my sister.

"How did you get her home Lina? We have tried everything. The priestesses and the muses have done every spell and ritual they could find." He questioned her.

"I did not do it. She did. When the Royal Moon rose in the

other realm, she cast the portal spell and I was waiting on the other side to pull her through. I knew she would be coming home today as soon as I saw the sun rise this morning. So I rode out to the clearing and waited until the portal opened."

"But what if you had been sucked through like your sister? This kingdom would not have survived losing another princess." My father said sadly.

"I did not care for my self, with my little sister stuck over there going through goddess knows what. I figured it was a risk worth taking if I had the chance to give this kingdom back their missing princess, and I wanted my sister back." Catalina explained.

"Well I for one am thankful your sister has finally returned to us." Michael said to Catalina as I smiled up at him.

"Yes you have been waiting very patiently, since she disappeared on the eve of your wedding day." Lina teased him.

"Speaking of which!" My mother said.

Everyone in the room turned to Mother as they always do when their queen speaks. She looked as if she had aged much in the 3 years I had been away. There were worry lines surrounding her eyes and covering her forehead, and her hair had started to gray. Despite all that, she still looked just as beautiful as she did when I left.

"Anastasia, I can give you a little time to get settled back in to life here, but we must start preparing for your wedding as soon as possible. The people will be ecstatic when word gets out that you have returned, but until your wedding takes place, they will not be able to move on." My mother said gently to me.

"I understand Mother. I do not need any time. I have waited three years for my wedding day. I will wait only long enough to get everything set up. The full moon will start to wan in 2 days. Is that enough time to prepare the wedding?" I declared as Michael gripped my hand in his.

"If that is what you wish, then I shall make it happen my dear." Mother smiled as she called one of the servants to her. After a whispered conversation, the servant rushed off to do whatever task my mother gave her.

By this time, we had all finished our meals and the servants were bringing out dessert. All I could smell, even before they stepped into the room, was the delicious strawberry and crème truffles the servants carried to us.

"Oh how I missed these!" I stated as I took my first bite of a childhood favorite that the other realm sadly lacked. Lina and Michael laughed at me as I devoured my dessert in a very unladylike manner.

The door opened as the servants were taking our empty plates. Much to my surprise, in walked my childhood best friend. She was followed by the royal florist and my mother's favorite seamstress. As Lysandra's eyes found me she gasped and her feet stopped. I jumped up from my seat and ran to her, much like my mother did when I made my entrance. I threw my arms around her and cried.

"Lysa I have missed you so much!" I said as I pulled back.

"I cannot believe you are here!" She exclaimed, her facing showing just as much surprise as her voice.

"Thank you all for coming so quickly." My mother called out. As she spoke, I took my cue to head back to my seat. Once I was seated, she continued. "As you can see, Princess Anastasia has returned to us. That being said, Lysandra you will return to your position as her handmaiden and will coordinate the details and preparation of her wedding. Sarah, I need you to work with Lysandra to make sure the throne room and this room are properly decorated. Shealah, I need you to prepare her wedding gown. The wedding is to take place in two days, and everything must be perfect! This will not only be a royal wedding, but also the first time the people see their long lost princess in three years." Lysandra and Sarah both accepted their tasks and stepped aside to start making plans. Shealah looked over at me.

"Your Highness, if I am to prepare your gown for the wedding in two days, I will need to see you tonight to get your measurements." She said softly.

"That is fine. I will come with you now. I am finished eating and I am sure anything else my family needs of me tonight can wait a little while." I said as I stood up. Michael kissed my hand before releasing me.

"I will be waiting when you are through." He whispered to me.

Shealah and I walked out together. Once we were out of earshot of my mother, she turned to me and looked me over.

"You do not seem to have changed much. You are a little

taller and broader but that is expected after three years." She stated plainly.

"Yes. I made sure that despite the difference in culture, I did not slip from the way we eat here and I kept very active." I responded politely.

We stepped into my dressing chambers and once we were alone, Shea dropped the formalities. No one in my family or in the palace staff knew of our relationship, except for Michael.

"It is good to see you Ana." She said with a smile as she searched for a measuring tape. "It is good to see you too Shea!" I said with a little more happiness. She started taking my measurements.

As she finished up she said, "As I said earlier, you haven't changed much. I will need to lengthen your dress but that should be it, since it is strapless."

"Thank you Shea! This means a lot!" I told her honestly. Usually your mistress is not the one making your wedding gown, but seeing as how I chose my mother's seamstress, she was kinda stuck in an awkward spot.

"It is not a big deal. I was asked by my queen so I must obey. Oh lets get you out of those clothes and into something proper." She said as she turned to sift through my wardrobe.

Ten minutes later, I walked around the corner towards my bedroom and almost ran into someone I did not recognize coming out of my room.

"Excuse me. Who are you?" I asked as she looked up at me

in surprise.

"Your Highness! It is true! You have returned!" She exclaimed.

"Yes I have returned. Now who are you and why are you coming from my bedroom?" I demanded getting angry that she did not answer the first time I asked. Did being gone for three years change how people acted around me?

"Oh I am sorry Your Highness. My name is Meagahn. I am Michael's sister in law. His brother wanted me to bring him a message." She explained sweetly.

"Nathaniel is married? Since when?" I asked dumbfounded. Michael's younger brother did not seem like he was interested in women or settling down the last time I saw him.

"About two years ago we wed. Last summer I gave birth to our first child and last week he fell ill. This morning his fever finally broke and Nathaniel bid me come tell his brother the good news." She answered happily.

"Oh that is wonderful news! I cannot wait to meet your little boy. Have you heard our news?" I exclaimed getting excited to have my old life back.

"No Your Highness. I have not." "We will have our wedding in two days time! You and your family must be there!"

"Oh that is wonderful news! Nathaniel will be so happy! Well I must get back to my son. Have a good night Your Highness!" She said as she stepped around me to leave.

Walking into my bedroom, I was greeted with the lovely

sight of my fiance half-naked on my bed. "I heard you talking to Meagahn, so I figured I would get comfy." He said as he got up and pulled me into his arms.

"Oh, how I have missed you my love! You do not know how long I searched all over the realm for a way to bring you home to me." He exclaimed as he started tearing up. It seemed like it would be a night of tears from everyone.

"It is okay. I am home now! And we will be wed once and for all in two days' time." I reassured him as I kissed him softly.

"I cannot wait two days. I need you now. Will you let me have you just two days before you are my wife?" He asked quietly as if he were afraid of my answer.

"I have spent three years not only waiting to be your wife, but also for you to take me as your own forever. I will wait no longer. The rules be damned. If the Goddess did not want us to be together yet, she would not have allowed us to want it so badly." I said quickly before smothering him with my lips. He managed to get my dress off without me even realizing it. After laying me on the bed, he stripped his clothes off and joined me.

Chapter Two

I awoke the next morning feeling as if I could finally relax. I was home with my parents and my big sister. I had the love of my life beside me. I was getting married tomorrow night. And that's when I realized, I would not relax until after the wedding. Lysandra would keep me on my toes with the wedding preparations and Shealah would be hounding me for fittings. And if that were not bad enough, Mother would go crazy if I did not give her a rundown of everything that has happened to me these last three years. As if she needed to reinforce my thoughts, Lysandra knocked on the door.

"I am sorry Stasia, but we need your approval on floral choices before I can start having the men decorate." She apologized sweetly.

"I understand. Give me five minutes to dress and I shall meet you in the banquet hall. That way I can eat breakfast while we work." I said with a smile. She nodded her head and left.

I ran down to my dressing chambers and started sifting through my wardrobe. I finally found my old favorite dress. I was stunned to see it fit perfectly despite me being taller. I had such fun finally dressing as the princess I was born to be. My dresses and jewels were my obsession as a child and living the last three years without them was torture.

When I finally walked into the banquet hall a few minutes later, I was dressed like a typical princess. I wore my favorite purple dress that I had accented with my silver jeweled belt around my waist. I adorned my neck and ears with the diamond set my grandmother had passed on to me. Weaved into my hair was the amethyst circlet Mother had given to me the day I was named Heiress. And to top it all off, I wore a new pair of silvery heels Lina had left in my room this morning. I was finally where I belonged, and I felt amazing.

The servants rushed to get me breakfast while Lysandra showed me the floral arrangements for the centerpieces. There were six different options and while I was trying to choose one of them, Sarah brought in the floral options for the throne room. I had never seen so many flowers in one room before. You could tell Mother was going all out for this.

After about an hour, I had finally decided on the centerpieces, the throne room decor, my bouquet, and the flower petals that would follow my steps down the aisle. As I sat down to breathe, Michael walked in.

"Good morning my love!" He smiled at me as a servant rushed off to get him something to eat. You could feel the happiness radiating off of him.

"Good morning!" I smiled back at him.

"I do not want to rush you away, but Shealah stopped by your room. She wants to see you as soon as you have a minute. She said she stayed up all night to work on your gown and wants to make sure she got the length right before she starts adding on some extra decoration she thought of." Michael relayed to me sadly.

"Alright. I am done here and have already eaten. I will go see her and hopefully after, we will have a minute to ourselves." I reassured him before kissing him and heading out the door.

I headed out to find Shealah. Mother said she saw her heading into my dressing chambers with my gown, so I headed that way. Outside the door to my dressing room my father stopped me.

"There you are Stasia. I have been looking everywhere for you." He said slightly out of breath.

"I am sorry Father. I was in the banquet hall taking care of wedding preparations." I apologized.

"Oh of course. I should have known."

"Is everything alright Father?" I asked a little worried. Father does not usually search us out himself. That is what he pays the servants for.

"Oh right. We received word from some farmers that the portal was seen opening this morning." He answered.

"What? Did anyone come through?" I asked starting to freak out. If someone had followed me from the other realm, it would not be good.

"They did not see anyone but I wanted to warn you and ask you if anyone over there knew how to open the portal." He reassured.

"I never told anyone where I came from. No one over there would have believed me but I guess someone might have found my spell book and tried out the portal spell. I have no idea who it would have been though. I kept mostly to myself because I was too busy trying to find a way home."

"Alright. I will send some guards to check it out just to make sure nothing came through." He said before kissing my cheek and walking away.

I took a deep breath to calm my thoughts and my racing heart, then walked into my dressing room. Shealah was standing in front of a full-length mirror she must have brought with her. Draped over the mirror was my wedding gown. Seeing it again after all this time, I almost started crying. I could not believe I would finally get to wear it the next day.

"Good morning Shea." I said softly as she had not seemed to notice my entrance yet. She jumped slightly and turned to me with a smile.

"Good morning Ana. Did you have a good night?" She questioned me teasingly. Shea is the only person who would not freak out over the fact that I let Michael take me as his before we were wed, seeing how her and I had slept together years ago.

"Yes I had quite a wonderful night. What about you?" I asked to change the topic but also to find out how she has been doing since I had been gone.

"Oh it was lovely. I stayed up all night working on your gown but was visited by a young man who is determined to win my heart." She told me matter of factly.

"Oh. Is this man worthy of your heart?" I asked, wanting

more details.

"According to my father he is. I am the royal seamstress and he is a royal guard. But I barely know him and I do not want to worry that my husband may one day have to go off to battle and not return."

"Who's guard is he in?" I asked curiously. Maybe I know the guy. My sister and I did grow up with most of the younger guards.

"He was in your guard before you disappeared and then your father transferred him to your sister."

"Oh? What is his name?"

"James. He is the son of your father's highest guard." James was after my mistress. Oh this would play out well. James and I had a thing as kids before I met Michael or Shea. I think my face gave away my thoughts. Shea looked at me like she just found out the man she was in love with was her brother.

"You know him then Ana?" She asked.

"Yes I do. We had a thing before I met you or Michael. He is a really good guy, and loyal. You would do well as his wife." I told her gently. She nodded like she already knew what I said.

Our conversation was changed back to focus on me, while she helped me into my gown. I spun around in front of the mirror admiring her handy work. It felt so good to be wearing my gown again. The silk clung to my curves perfectly and the lace draped the skirt like freshly fallen snow on a frozen pond. She tightened the corset and tied it tight.

The bead work on it was astonishing. In the other realm they did all that with machines but here it was more beautiful knowing that someone had taken the time to stitch every single bead into its proper place by hand.

Shea examined the gown and how it fit. She walked around me a few times and then measured the bottom. After a few silent moments, she looked up at me with a smile.

"I knew this would be perfect! You look even more beautiful than usual Ana! I cannot wait to add the final touches I just thought of last night. Those will be a surprise. Once we leave here, you will not see your gown again until it's time to prepare for the wedding tomorrow night. But rest assured, I know what you like and you will love what I have in store for you!" Shea gushed as she started unlacing the corset.

"Thank you Shea! I know whatever you do, I will love it!" I gushed right back, finally feeling like a bride again.

Once I was back in my purple dress and all my jewels, I turned to Shea with a wicked grin. She stepped back and put her stuff down. She knew what that look meant. Three years apart had not changed anything about me.

"Have I told you how much I missed you Shea? I have not felt the tender touch of a woman in three years." I said as I slowly walked towards her. For each step I took towards her, she took one back. Finally I had her pinned in a corner.

Thankfully we were in my dressing room, the only room in the palace no one could enter without my permission. I brought my hands up to cup the sides of her face and gently stroked her neck. After what seemed like forever, I leaned in and kissed her. She knew the role of a mistress. She kissed me back but only following my moves. Her hands stayed by her sides as mine traveled over her body. When we kissed, it seemed like my hands had a mind of their own. They examined every inch of her torso, favoring her large breasts. A soft moan escaped her lips when my hands traveled down to cup her nice tight ass.

After a while of kissing and caressing, I pulled her down to the floor, on top of me. She knew what that meant. It was her turn to explore. But unlike me, she did not explore with her hands. She trailed light kisses from my lips, down my neck. She knew I loved it when she kissed my neck. A soft bite at the base of my throat pulled a moan out of me. She grinned as she continued. The kisses left my neck and traveled over my chest. Soon she had the neck of my dress down and was kissing my breasts. I cried out as the pleasure hit me when she sucked my nipple into her mouth. I had forgotten how good she was with her mouth. When I told her that, she chuckled before moving lower. She pushed my skirts up and trailed kisses up my legs. Once at the top, she paused and looked at me for her cue. I nodded, and she grinned before going back down and proving to me just how good with her mouth she was.

An hour later, I was walking through the gardens trying to find Michael. Rounding a corner, I was stopped by a large purple rose bush that wasn't there when I was here last. I saw a small plaque held by a goddess statue at the base of the bush. It read

"These flowers were planted in honor of Princess Anastasia, The Princess that was lost to time. May she find her way home." I was stunned. I knew everyone had been affected by my absence, but I was not expecting monuments. I started tearing up over it all, and that was when Michael decided to make an appearance.

"It was Shea's idea. About a year after you left, she came to me and said how surprised she was that the queen had not constructed some kind of monument in your honor yet. We discussed between the two of us what kind of monument you would like and finally came to the agreement that as long as it was purple and nature based you would be happy." He informed me as he stood beside me. He wiped the tears from my face and kissed me softly.

"It is beautiful." I said softly.

"I wanted it to be as beautiful as the woman it honored." I had always loved the way he turned everything into a compliment on my beauty. We started walking back inside.

The castle was bustling with activity. Everyone was working to get it ready for the wedding. Just inside the doors Michael pulled me to a stop. "What is wrong love?" I asked him concerned.

"Before you went to the gardens, where were you? You were gone for a couple hours." He asked me curiously.

"I am sorry. I went to meet Shea for my fitting." I looked around to make sure no one was within earshot, then continued, "We got a little distracted." He smiled and nodded.

"Of course you did. I was wondering how long it would take for you to reconnect. How does that work after we are married?" He asked.

"It works however we want it to, but it seems she may be off the market soon."

"Oh really?"

"Yes. She informed me one of my old guards is pursuing her. Her father approves but she is wary. She does not like the idea of her husband going off to battle and possibly not coming home to her. I understand her concern, but I gave her my blessing. He is a good guy and would be a loving husband."

"Which guard is it?"

"James" I told him absently.

"Ah okay. They would make a cute couple. Maybe I should give him some advice on how to win her heart." He said as if he were an expert. He forgets our marriage had been arranged. Us falling in love before we married had just been an added benefit.

"You can try." I laughed at him.

"I will, after the wedding. So what would you like to do now?"

"I want to relax for as long as my family and staff will allow." He grinned at me before leading me off down a corridor that looked familiar but I couldn't place it.

Michael opened the door at the end of the corridor to reveal a much expanded version of my favorite room in the castle. The walls of the library were lined floor to ceiling with books and all of the book cases throughout the room were filled to bursting point. The room had been added on to. Before I left, there was only about ten book cases. Now there were almost fifty.

I stood in the doorway in awe. He pulled me into the room and over to a circle of lounge chairs placed in front of a burning hearth. He laid down on a chair and pulled me down with him. Once we got comfortable, he picked up a book off the center table and started reading to me. I had always loved listening to him read. His deep masculine voice just made every book and poem sound that much more magical. The book he happened to pick up was the one we were reading when I left. He even started from the exact spot we left off at.

It felt good being able to lay here with him and continue with our life as if the last three years had not happened. I knew if anyone was going to treat me like this it would be him. He truly was the perfect match for me.

My mother had arranged our marriage when we were ten. He was the eldest son of her favorite Lord, so naturally he would be her choice to marry her heiress. We met at my tenth birthday ball, when my mother announced our engagement. At first I was pissed that she would do this without even telling me, but then we danced. Our first dance was to my favorite song and the entire dance he stared directly into my eyes. I, being a stubborn princess, stared right back. In his eyes I saw nothing but honesty and trustworthiness. He did not speak once until the end of the dance. He bowed to me and kissed my hand. Then he said

"I look forward to our next dance my queen." And that is when my heart screamed at me not to let him go. After the dance I had Lysa slip him a note telling him to meet me in the gardens. When he arrived, I was seated on a bench staring up at the stars. He sat down next to me and just watched me in silence until I spoke.

"Mother expects us to marry on my fifteenth birthday. That means we will have this year to get to know one another and then on my eleventh birthday, you will move into the palace. You will have four years to get accustomed to palace life before our wedding. How do you feel about that?" I had asked him.

"As long as it ends with you as my wife, I will do whatever your mother wants." He had responded without hesitation.

"Why?"

"Because our parents wish us to marry, and no one says no to your mother. But also because I have loved you since I first saw you two years ago at your sister's birthday ball. You walked in an hour late, wearing a shiny blue gown. Your hair was messy like you had just come in from a ride on your horse to discover the ball and your mother chastised you for it in front of everyone. You were angered and embarrassed yet all I saw was beauty. From that moment on, I prayed that the Goddess would bring us together." I had kissed him then, and from that moment on we were inseparable until the night before my fifteenth birthday.

I had gone out for a ride with Lina to get rid of some of the pent up energy and excitement over my wedding the next day. We were riding out near the farmland on the outskirts of the castle grounds. All of a sudden, the space in front of me opened up into a purple portal and I was pulled through by some unseen force. The last thing I saw before it closed was Lina running towards me screaming. My new surroundings were much different than I was used to, but I adapted as much as I could while also searching for some way to return home to my family and my fiance.

It took two years, but one day I had stumbled across an old spellbook that was all about portal travel. I read it cover to cover multiple times, before I finally had enough information to construct the spell I needed to open a portal back to my realm. The only issue was I had to wait for the Royal Moon, a full moon that shone brightly through a purple haze, which only happens once every fifty years. Luckily for me, I did not have to wait that long. The next Royal Moon was to happen right after my birthday the following year.

Michael pulled me from my thoughts when he put the book down. He looked down at me and smiled.

"You have no idea what just happened do you?" He teased.

"I am sorry. I was thinking about the first time we met and everything that has happened since." I apologized.

"Oh. I think about that day often. It has been my favorite day for years. It helped me get through the worst days without you. But your sister just came in looking for you. I guess your mother wants you."

"Oh damn. I was comfortable." I said as I sat up. He laughed at me as he stood up with me.

We walked hand in hand as he lead me to the throne room. There were men and women all over the place, setting it up for our wedding, but Mother sat up front on her throne as if the hustle and bustle all around her was not happening. She smiled as she saw us approach and gestured the servant she had been talking to away.

"Finally. Anastasia where have you been?" She asked me as we finally reached her.

"I am sorry Mother. Michael and I were relaxing in the library." I told her as I took a seat on my throne for the first time in three years. "

Ah alright. Well at least you finally emerged. I heard the fitting went well this morning with Shealah." She said conversationally.

"Yes. The dress still fit wonderfully. She had to lengthen it last night so it would be long enough. Shealah said she had some surprise additions she was adding to it today, so I am excited to see it tomorrow night." I told my mother, sounding every bit the excited bride.

"So I hate to do this to you Anastasia, but I need to know what happened over the last three years while you were gone." Mother said apologetically.

"I understand Mother." I said before delving into a rundown of everything I had done and gone through since I left.

Three hours later, we were sitting in the banquet hall eating dinner. Father and Michael were talking about my guard detail and trying to acquire new guards. Mother and Catalina were discussing some issues some of the farmers were having. And that left me alone with my thoughts. I was finally home, finally complete, and I could not wait to see what the future had in store for me.

Chapter Three

I awoke the morning of my wedding to Catalina jumping on my bed. I swear sometimes she forgets she is twenty years old. "Oh calm down Lina. You are going to cause an earthquake." I chastised as I sat up with a smile.

"Oh hush. Mother sent me to see why you missed breakfast." She informed me.

"I missed breakfast? What time is it?" I asked confused. I never slept in. It just wasn't in my nature.

"It is an hour before midday meal."

"Oh my goddess! Is mother upset? What have I missed?" I exclaimed, even more shocked at myself.

"She is more worried than upset. She thought maybe the traveling between realms had made you ill. You did not miss much. The staff is almost finished preparing the palace for your wedding and Father and Michael have been busy testing the applicants for your new guard. They have been out in the courtyard since dawn with all the men. I think you will have the largest guard in history." She laughed as I rolled my eyes at her. "Have you heard anything from Shealah? Is my gown ready? I am dying to see it!" I asked getting excited since my wedding was only a few hours away.

"No I have not. No one has heard anything from her since she left the palace last night. I am sure she is just busy making sure your gown is perfect." She reassured me happily, but I noticed the hint of sadness in her voice.

I knew my sister was forcing all the positivity. She is the eldest, so naturally she should be the heiress. She should have been married five years ago. I had been given her birthright, when it was discovered that Catalina could not have children. It killed me to take it from her, but the people needed to have a queen that could provide an heir. And according to our laws, a woman who could not bare children, could not marry. So my sister had lost not only her chance at the throne, but also her chance at a happy life with a husband to love and cherish her. The day Mother crowned me her Heiress, I had made a promise to my sister, that one day I would find a way to at least give her a happy life. We both knew I could not give her the throne, but I could try to change the law so she could one day marry.

Lina realized that I caught the sadness in her voice and turned her head away. I pulled her into my arms and hugged her. "You remember what I promised you right Lina?" I whispered softly.

"Yes but it does not matter. I will never find a man willing to marry a woman who could not give him children, even if that woman was a princess." She said sadly as a tear escaped down her face.

"There is someone out there for you. We just have to find him, and me getting married tonight will put us one step closer to you getting married. You know I will be taking the throne as soon as my first child is born. Once I am Queen, I will have the ability to change the law, allowing you to marry."

"I love your determination Stasia. Now lets get you ready for your big day! I will not allow my sorrows to ruin my little sister's wedding!" She exclaimed as she jumped off my bed wiping her eyes.

Half an hour later, we were walking into the banquet hall. Everything was in place for my wedding feast tonight. The hall looked beautiful, decorated with every kind of purple flower you could imagine. There was a decoration I did not expect in the center of the room. It was a marble statue of Michael and I. We looked like gods. The artist did a remarkable job capturing every feature of our bodies, while also making the statues look heaven-sent.

"Mother had it commissioned. She said it will be placed in front of the palace after tonight." Lina told me as the actual Michael stepped out from behind the statue.

"Ah there you are my love! I was about to come searching for you." He said with a smile.

"I am sorry. I guess I overslept, and then Lina and I were talking after she shook me awake." I informed him before kissing him softly.

"Oh well at least you finally awoke. It would not have been good for you to sleep through our wedding." He teased.

"Do not worry. Nothing will stop us from marrying

tonight." I said, letting every ounce of my determination set my oath in stone.

"Good. Oh Shealah is waiting for you in your dressing room. She said the gown is finished but before you get to see it, she needs to figure out how you want your hair and such." He informed me sounding very much like a man.

"Wonderful! I will head over there right away! Lina you are coming with me right?" I asked my sister, getting very excited!

"Of course!"

Ten minutes later, we walked into my dressing room to find Shealah talking with Lysandra, my mother, and an older woman I did not recognize. Upon our entrance, the conversation halted. Everyone looked at us like they were not sure what to say or do.

"What happened? What is wrong?" I asked seeing my mother's eyes filled with tears.

"Girls sit down." She said softly. Lina and I listened to our mother as we shared a look of fear and confusion. This was supposed to be a happy day. I was getting married that evening. I could not figure out what would cause my mother to look at us like that on the morning of my wedding, but then her next words made my heart break and Lina screamed. "An hour ago your father went out with some guards to check into the portal opening that the farmers had reported yesterday. Some of the guards came back a few minutes ago. Your father was not among them. A farmer just arrived right before I came in here. He had brought his wagon to the back entrance of the palace. Inside was your father's body."

"That is not possible." I managed to say despite my throat going dry and my heart seeming to have stopped. Mother dropped to her knees in front of us and wrapped her arms around us. That's when I knew it was true, because the queen was never found on her knees. At this moment, she was not the queen of this kingdom. She was our mother, and a grieving wife.

"I need to see him." I said over my sister's sobs.

A few minutes later, Lina and I walked into our father's office. In front of the hearth, there was a small bed, and on the bed lay our father's body, still and cold. Lina dropped to her knees right there in the doorway. I walked slowly up to him. As I stared down at him, I started crying. I had just gotten my family back after three years of being away from them, and now here my father was in front of me, dead. He was supposed to give me away tonight at my wedding, but instead he would be burning on his funeral pyre. All I could think was, how did this happen? How did my father die? Then it hit me. Someone did come through that portal yesterday, and they were no friend.

I ran out of the room, unable to look at him any longer. This was my fault. Someone had followed me back here and they had killed my father. It was my fault he was dead, my fault my mother no longer had a husband, my fault my sister no longer had a father, my fault this kingdom no longer had a king. I collapsed in the middle of a hallway. I couldn't control the sobs or the self hatred. I have no idea how long I sat there like that, but after some time, Michael dropped to his knees in front of me and pulled me into his arms.

"I am so sorry my love! I am so sorry!" He kept saying over and over again as he rocked me. When I could speak again, I looked up at him and said, "Why are you sorry? This is my fault! I killed him!"

"This is not your fault Ana. Someone killed him out in the fields. The entire guard is out looking for his killer. They will find him." Michael tried to reassure me.

"No it is my fault. Whoever killed my father, followed me back here from the other realm. I pretty much left the door open for them to come through, and now my father is dead because of it."

"It is not your fault. Your father was not supposed to go out there himself. That is what the guards are for, but he wanted to make sure that nothing went wrong for our wedding tonight, so he decided to check it out himself."

"That just proves my point Michael. He died to make sure MY wedding went perfect. Now it won't be perfect. My father will not be there, so not only is his death my fault, but he died in vain." I could not help myself. I pushed him away and started walking down the hall. He of course followed me.

I ended up outside the throne room when he decided to stop me. He turned me towards him and kissed me.

"None of this is your fault. And you need to stop making yourself believe that. You are a princess and the next queen of this kingdom. I know you are grieving the loss of your father, but you need to pull yourself together. Your mother and sister are going to need you. They have no one else. This kingdom needs you. The people need to see that they still have a strong ruler, and you know if your mother needs to, she can step aside for a while to grieve in private. That will give you her responsibilities. I will also not allow this killer to ruin our wedding. Yes, your father will not be able to give you away, but he will still be there in spirit, and if you remember that, then it will go wonderfully. The people will know the royal family is still here for them, and we will finally be wed." I looked up at him with a sad smile.

"You are right my love. I am sorry. I do not know how I let myself get like that. I am usually the strong one. I need to find my mother and Lina."

Michael and I searched for my mother and sister. Finally, after almost an hour, we found them in the garden. I hugged Lina as Michael went up to my mother and embraced her gently saying, "I am so sorry Madame."

"Thank you, Michael. At least we have each other to help us get through this difficult time." Mother said softly.

"Mother we need to discuss what we are going to do." I said, forcing myself to hold back my emotions.

"Yes of course. What were you thinking Anastasia?" She said sounding more like herself.

"We still have plenty of time this afternoon to have Father's funeral before the wedding. So I think we should send some servants to get everything ready in the courtyard. Also, if you need sometime to yourself, I can step in and give you as much time as you need."

"You are still going to have your wedding tonight?" Catalina asked, her voice sounding very hoarse from all of her crying.

"Of course. You were there when I swore to Michael this morning, that I would not let anything delay our wedding any longer. And the people need it. They need to see that we are still here for them even while we are dealing with such a loss." Mother was nodding, as I spoke, as if to give her support to what I was saying.

"She is right Catalina. Yes we all need to take time to grieve in our own ways, but we cannot allow our heartache to take a toll on our kingdom. Anastasia, I think you are right about how we should do things today, and I would greatly appreciate it if you could take over for a little while. Michael, could you send some servants to setup the funeral?"

"Of course Madame." Michael said before leaving to do what he was asked.

An hour later, everyone was gathered in the main courtyard. Father's body had been placed on his pyre, and I was standing in front of it speaking to the crowd. I spoke of

Father and his many achievements, his love for the people, and his love for his family. After I was done speaking, I discovered who the mystery woman was in my dressing room when Mother told us of Father's death. She was his older sister Analysa. We had not seen her since we were children, so it was not a surprise that I had not recognized her. She went up with Mother to light Father's pyre. Once the flames start roaring, I dismissed everyone.

Shealah came up to me as everyone was leaving and lead me off to my dressing room. Once inside, she pulled me into a tight embrace. It felt so good to have her arms around me, and after holding in my emotions the last few hours, I could not anymore. I started crying into her hair.

"Oh no you do not. Our next queen cannot have tear stained cheeks as she marries the love of her life. I will not allow it. Now wipe those eyes or you will not be able to see the hard work I have put into your gown." Despite my best efforts, I ended up laughing at her as she threw a handful of tissues in my face before going to my wardrobe and pulling out my gown.

The gown was gorgeous. Her extra little touches really were perfect. She had added purple stitching into the seems of the corset and replaced the white ribbon with a purple one. The lace that draped the skirt was a soft lilac which matched the corset ribbon. She also added a veil made from the same lace she put over the skirt.

I was speechless. All I could do was pull her into my arms and hug her tightly. She kissed my cheek softly.

"You will look so beautiful tonight. Your father will be crying in the heavens." She said as I let her go.

"Thank you Shea!" I managed to say with a smile.

She helped me into the gown. As she was lacing up the corset, my mother and sister came in. My mother was speechless as she took me in. Catalina walked up to me with a smile.

"You look beautiful Stasia." She said as my mother wiped the tears off her face.

"I wish your father was here to see you Anastasia." Mother said softly.

"He is here Mother. Father will never leave us. We may not be able to see him, but if we allow ourselves, we can feel his presence." I reassured her.

Catalina did my hair, while Mother searched for the perfect jewels. Finally, twenty minutes before I was supposed to walk down the aisle, I was ready. My hair was set perfectly with my veil held in with gorgeous amethyst clips my sister had got for me. My gown was the most beautiful gown I had ever seen, and I felt my father's presence beside me.

Everyone left me to go find their places in the throne room. I took a few moments to myself, to collect myself. Then I walked down to the throne room as well. I stood outside the main doors, waiting for the moment they would open and my wedding would begin.

The music began and the doors opened. As I came into view, the room was silent except for the music playing softly in the background. As I stepped forward, I had eyes for no one except Michael. He stood in front of the thrones, dressed in a brand-new suit. He looked even more handsome than usual, but I knew it was just because we were finally here at this moment, the moment we had waited so long for. He smiled at me as I walked towards him. As I got closer he looked me over. "You are the most beautiful woman in existence." He whispered to me as he took my hand.

We turned toward the High Priestess and she began the ceremony. It was not a very long ceremony, but it was powerful. After we said our vows and we turned towards the crowd for the priestess to proclaim us husband and wife, I saw just how much the people needed this today.

After our first kiss as husband and wife, we led the procession into the banquet hall for the feast. We sat at the center of the head table, where on normal days my parents would sit. My mother and sister were seated with us. It started out just as perfect as the ceremony. We ate a wonderful meal, and before dessert, Michael and I had our first dance as husband and wife. As the dance ended, we took our seats. The servants started bringing out dessert, but as we started eating ours, we all heard loud noises coming from the hall.

A moment later the doors burst open, and Father's head guard came walking in. He walked right up to me and bowed. "I am sorry to interrupt Your Highness, but I have something that needs your attention right away." He stated. I put my fork down and took a sip of my wine.

"What is it sir?" I asked.

"We have found your father's murderer." He said slowly. The whole room gasped. Michael grabbed my hand as I looked over at my mother. She nodded to me.

"Bring him in here." I commanded.

Without hesitation, the guards dragged in their prisoner. They threw him at my feet and Father's guard pulled his head up so I could see who he was. Staring up at me was none other than the one person from the other realm I had actually considered a friend. Marcus and I had met my first day there. He helped me adjust to being in a new place. He did not know where I truly came from, but he helped me with anything I needed. We had become very close in the three years I had been there, to the point where I had considered starting a life with him if I could never get back home.

Now he was in chains at my feet because he had killed my father on the morning of my wedding. The anger flared up inside me. I stood up and was about to walk around the table to him, when Michael grabbed my hand. I knew he noticed the recognition in my eyes when I looked at Marcus, and he saw the hatred and betrayal there now. He was trying to keep me from going too far in front of my people.

With Mother stepping aside to grieve, I was responsible for dealing with Father's killer. I had to be a queen now, not a grieving daughter, or a betrayed friend. I turned my gaze away from Marcus and looked out at my people.

"My people, we have all been through a lot today. We awoke to the news of our King's untimely death, on the day of his daughter's wedding. We sat through the funeral of our King and the wedding of our next Queen. Our emotions are running wild right now, but I stand before you now, to declare that we will all go to sleep this night knowing that our King's murderer has been brought to justice. This man before you will breath one more night, and as the sun rises tomorrow morning, I will watch as the man I once called a friend pays the price for taking the life of my father." I looked down at Marcus with my last words and saw as his eyes went wide. He had no idea until then that the man he had killed was my father. He had no idea who I was here, or the power I have.

"Please Stasia. I didn't mean to. I was defending myself. I am so sorry." Marcus called out.

"How dare you speak to the princess." One of the guards yelled at him, "How dare you use her name."

"Shane, it is okay. Marcus here can say whatever he likes,

but it will help him not, for I have the final say with the matter of my father's death, and as I said a moment ago, he will take his last breath at sunrise. I will give my mother and my sister, and our people the satisfaction of watching the life drain from his eyes." I said to the guard to calm him, "Now take the prisoner to a cell. I will finish my dessert and then pay him a little visit before retiring for the night. After all this is still my wedding."

After I had my fill of the feast and everyone gushing about the wedding while also giving their condolences, I said good night to everyone. I headed to the wing of the castle where the cells are. I just had to talk to him and find out what was going on. Him being here did not make any sense. Marcus was nice and everything in the other realm, but he did not seem like a stalker.

Once I was outside his cell, I realized Michael was still with me. I did not want him around when I spoke with Marcus.

"Could you give me a few moments to speak with the prisoner alone, my love? I will meet you in our room when I am done." I asked sweetly, knowing he wished I would wait until tomorrow so we could spend our wedding night the way it was supposed to be.

"Are you sure you want to be alone with him?" Michael asked, sounding more concerned for me than I expected.

"Yes I am fine. I have gotten used to pushing my feelings aside to do what was needed today." He nodded and then kissed me before turning and heading back towards our room.

I took a deep breath before entering the cell. I looked around and Marcus was still chained. He sat in the corner, curled up with his knees to his face. As I entered, he looked over at me and his eyes widened. He tried to stand up but the chains held him in place. "Stasia I am so sorry. Please forgive me. I had no idea he was your father." Marcus started saying.

"Silence." I stopped him before he could keep going. I did not want to hear that he was sorry. His apologies would not bring my father back.

"I may have been a lost and lonely girl back when we met, but here I am powerful. I am the daughter and heiress of the queen. I am acting ruler while my mother grieves the loss of her husband. Here I am looked up to by every person alive. I will not listen to your apologies or your excuses. Even in your own world, they would not do you well. If you had killed a man in your realm, you would be arrested and possibly put to death, depending on where you lived. Here you are at my mercy. I hold all the cards now, and I am here for one reason only. I want to know why you came here and how. Answer me truthfully, and I may give you a painless death. Lie to me, and you will wish I killed you quickly." I demanded, sounding very much like my mother.

Marcus was stunned. He sat in silence for a few minutes,

trying to gather his thoughts. Finally he spoke, "I was watching as you cast the spell to bring yourself home. I had known for a while that you would be leaving soon, but I kept hoping I could change your mind. Over the time we spent together, I had grown to love you. I knew it was useless because your heart belonged to another, but I couldn't help myself. Then seeing you go through the portal, I wanted to follow you and try to win your heart. I recreated the spell you had used, with a few modifications to the incantation, and it worked. I stepped through the portal and found myself in a field. That was when I realized, I had no clue how I was going to find you here. You had never told me anything about your life. So I hid in the field and tried to come up with a plan. The next thing I knew there were guards all around me. I tried running, but one caught me. We started to fight and when he swung his sword at me, I managed to twist it just right for it to get him instead of me. When he went down, all the other men froze, so I booked it. I had no idea who the man was, just that his death was my fault."

I stared at him shocked for only a moment. I had not expected this to be about love. As he said, my heart belonged to another and the way I was raised, is when someone belongs to one person, no one goes after them. I forgot that it is not that way where Marcus comes from. I pulled myself together and looked him dead in the face.

"Thank you for your honesty. I will see you at sunrise." I said before standing up and leaving.

Chapter Four

Walking into my room a few minutes later, I was stunned. My room had been transformed. There were rose petals covering the floor. Bouquets sat in half the windows, candles in the other half. Michael laid in the middle of our bed, completely naked. He had a wicked grin on his face, one that made me shiver with anticipation.

After my inspection of the room, he walked over to me and kissed me. He had never kissed me like that before. It was gentle and filled with love but yet forceful and filled with passion at the same time. As we kissed, he undid the ribbon for my corset and removed my gown. Pressing me against the door, his lips moved from mine down to my neck as his hands cupped my breasts. I could feel him harden as he pressed himself against me. "Michael" I moaned softly.

"Yes my bride?" he whispered softly into my ear. "No more teasing, my love. I am yours. Take me." I demanded.

As if my words had flipped a switch inside him, his actions changed dramatically. He lifted me up, wrapping my legs around his waist. Unlike the night before, he did not enter me gently. This was our wedding night, and he was not holding back. He made love to me against the door to our bedroom. Every thrust was just as forceful as the first. By the time he brought me over the edge, two hours had passed and he did not seem to be losing any stamina.

He finished against the door and carried me to the bed. Once I was lying down, he started all over again. It seemed his second wind was stronger than the first. Michael moved as if he had been waiting his entire life for this moment. Every time he pushed inside me, his eyes filled with success. I could not get enough of him.

After he was done, I decided to change it up.

"Let me do something for you now, my love." I said sweetly, before flipping us around. Once I was on top, I rode him as if my life depended on it. His moans were all the push I needed. I moved my body in ways I did not know I could.

By the time we finally finished, the sky was starting to lighten. There was a soft knock on the door.

"I guess its time to clean up." Michael laughed as he slipped his robe on and answered the door. A few minutes later, he turned back to me, the humor had left his face.

"Lysandra said that the guards have brought the prisoner to the courtyard. Everything is ready for you. I told her we would be there in ten minutes, so let's go get dressed."

As we walked out of the castle, I could see all of the people gathered to watch the execution. It was a much larger group than at my father's funeral or my wedding. It seemed that our people who did not live close by had had time to arrive. Mother was standing up front with Aunt Analysa beside her. Their arms were wrapped around each other, to support their broken hearts. Catalina stood a few feet away from my mother. One of her guards was with her, and she was crying into his shoulder. I made sure to make a mental note of that so I could ask Lina about it later. I turned the corner and there was Marcus, chained to the ground beside the spot where my father had burned on his funeral pyre. He looked right at me as I walked forward. His eyes filled with sadness. He had come here to chase love, and ended up killing himself.

I stood in front of him, facing the crowd. I took a moment to look out at everyone, trying to gather my thoughts. I sent a silent prayer to the Goddess, to guide my words and my actions. Immediately, I felt her presence within me. That gave me the extra push I needed to continue with what I was supposed to do.

"Ladies and Gentlemen, thank you for gathering this early in the morning. As you all know, this man behind me is the man who killed your king. After my wedding last night, I paid him a visit. I wanted to know how he had gotten here and why he had come. He told me that he was watching as I came through the portal and had recreated the spell I used. He came here to try and find me and win my heart. We had been friends while I was gone, and he knew that I belonged to another, but he did not care. His determination to win my heart has now cost us the life of our king and cost him his own life. With the Goddess's blessing, I have sentenced him to death, and now we will watch as his sentence is fulfilled." I spoke trying to sound as regal as I could.

As I finished my little speech, I felt the Goddess's presence shift. In front of me, she appeared in an ethereal form. She smiled at me, then walked over to Marcus. She pulled him up to his feet and looked him in the eyes.

"Marcus, you have taken the life of one of my children. I do not come here in person for many things, but the wrongful death of my children calls for it. I am here to fulfill your sentence." The Goddess spoke to him with a sad but powerful voice. When she finished speaking, she raised her hand to his chest and we all watched as her touch stopped his heart.

The Goddess caught Marcus's body and gently laid it on the ground before turning back to the people gathered in front of us. She looked out across the group of her children with a sad yet happy smile.

"My children, do not grieve. Your King watches over you all while sitting at my side. And since there must always be balance in the world, I am here to balance out his death. For each new death, there must also be new life. This new life will come to you in nine months time in the form of a little princess." With that said, The Goddess turned to me and

Michael. She took both our hands in hers and spoke to us. "
 You two have gone through a lot of heartbreak, and for that I am sorry, but without that heartbreak you would not be the strong leaders you are today. For your strength and love, I am leaving you with the gift of parenthood. Your first child will be born nine months from today. She will radiate grace and she will shine with the beauty of the Gods. And Anastasia, do not forget your promise, for the answer is right in front of you. Now I leave you all with my love."

Everyone was stunned by the bright light that appeared to bring the Goddess home, but as it dissipated the crowd broke up. Our people went on their way while they discussed the happenings this morning. Michael pulled me aside before I had a chance to move or even think. He brought me back into the garden near my rose bush. Before he spoke he pulled me into his arms and kissed me. I could feel his love flowing through me as his lips touched mine. "I love you Anastasia!" he said softly as he broke away from our kiss.

"I love you too Michael." I responded as I wiped a tear from my face.

"Are you okay my love?" He asked a little worried. His worry was warranted. I mean we did just watch as our goddess appeared and killed my best friend of the last three years the day after said best friend killed my father. Though despite all that, I was fine, wonderful actually.

"Yes Michael. I am okay. I'm just so happy and a little surprised honestly. Obviously I've always wanted and expected to have children but I was not expecting it to happen this quickly." Michael laughed at me.

"What do you mean quickly? We still have nine months to wait before she is born. And what did the Goddess mean by *'Do not forget your promise'?"*

"The day that Mother named me her heir, I swore to Catalina that once I was Queen I would make sure she got her happy ending. Even though I could not give her the throne, I would make sure she was able to marry and I would help her find the man of her dreams. Though if what the Goddess said is true, Lina might have already found him. I need to ask her about the guard she was standing with earlier." I explained to Michael and he looked dumbfounded. Obviously that was not what he expected to hear.

An hour or so later, I was sitting in one of the parlors waiting for Catalina to arrive for tea. This would be the first time I saw my sister since the Goddess's appearance. I wasn't sure how she was doing or what she thought of the Goddess's gift to us. To say I was nervous and anxious was an understatement. I kept fidgeting with the tea set laid out in front of me.

The door to the parlor opened and I never realized it until Catalina was seated in front me. She looked overjoyed, which both calmed me and made me more anxious. She took the teapot and poured us both a cup before taking a sip of hers.

"I am so excited for you Stasia! And for me! I cannot wait

to be an auntie!" She exclaimed after putting her cup back on the saucer. Her excitement was hard to fight. Before I knew it, I was just as excited.

"You will make a great auntie! But lets not talk about all that right now. You owe me some information Lina!"

Catalina looked honestly confused. I could see in her eyes that she had no idea what I was talking about. She sipped her tea and nibbled on one of the cookies while she tried to figure it out. I decided to take pity on her and explained what I meant.

"I saw you earlier at the execution. You were standing a few feet away from Mother and you were in the arms of one of your guards. You two looked quite comfortable in each others arms." To say she was shocked would be an understatement. She had no idea anyone had noticed them.

"We are just friends. He has been keeping me company since Father's death, making sure I was not alone. That is all." She spoke as if she had rehearsed that answer in her head many times, but I could tell that she wished their relationship was more.

"Before the Goddess left she told me not to forget my promise for the answer was right in front of me. Do you know what that means Lina?" I asked her getting excited.

"No." She responded automatically.

"It means that guard is the answer. He is the one you will marry once I am Queen and am able to change the law. You will have your happy ending Lina!" "How do you know he would be willing to marry me? Everyone knows I cannot have children and no man would want a wife that cannot give him children."

"Lina let me worry about that. Michael and I have our ways of making things work in our favor. If you want this man, he shall be yours. It is only a matter of when, not if." Lina jumped up and hugged me.

After Catalina and I finished our tea, I sent a servant to fetch Lina's guard. When he arrived in the parlor, he was confused as to why he was being summoned by me but he was respectful. He walked in and bowed to me before speaking.

"Your Highness, what is it you need from me?" He asked.

"Please have a seat." I said gesturing to the couch across from me. He sat down and was even more confused when I handed him a cup of tea. I smiled at him before sipping my own cup of tea.

"You are wondering why I called upon you in stead of one of my own guards. Let me be honest. This is not a matter between a Princess and a Guard. This is about a promise between two sisters that you may just be the answer to." I said mysteriously.

"I am sorry Your Highness. I do not understand." He responded softly.

"What do you think of my sister?" I asked and was surprised to see him blush.

"She is beautiful and kind. She usually puts everyone's needs before her own. She is a strong leader despite the fact that she is not the princess who will take the throne. Why do you ask?" I smiled at his response before answering his question.

"This may sound strange but bear with me. The day my mother crowned me her heiress, I made a promise to Catalina. I swore to her that once I was Queen, I would make sure she got her happy ending. Neither of us knew how I would keep this promise, until this morning. When the Goddess appeared at the execution, she spoke directly to me before leaving. She told me not to forget my promise for the answer was right in front of me. And when I looked in front of me, I saw my sister in your arms and you both looked quite content with staying like that."

"Your Highness, if it is allowed and your sister wants me, I am hers. My heart has belonged to her since we were young but at the time I stayed away because she was to be the next Queen and would end up marrying a Lord. Then it was discovered that she would not be able to take the throne for reasons that made it so she could not marry according to the current laws. At that time, I swore I would be there for Catalina in anyway she needed me." He declared, sounding just like Michael did every time he told me how much he loved me.

"Damyen obviously you know she cannot have children. This does not bother you at all?" I asked curious to hear how he would answer this. "Honestly Your Highness, I cannot have children either. So it would not be fair to marry a woman who could have children." He answered sounding as if he had never told this to anyone.

"Does Catalina know?"

"No she does not." "In that case, I think you need to tell her. And you have my permission as the next Queen of this kingdom to court her as long as you keep it quiet until I take the throne." I declared sounding very proud of myself and excited for my sister.

The next few days went by in a blur. Michael and I went to all the meetings that my parents would have normally taken care of. When we were not in meetings we were either in the library reading, or strolling through the gardens. Every time I saw Catalina, I could see how happy she was, which told me that Damyen had listened to me. Lina and I had not had a chance to talk since I had my conversation with Damyen but she had stopped me in the hall one day to give me a hug and whisper Thank you to me before heading off to where ever she was headed.

Chapter Five

Before I knew it, the days turned into weeks and the weeks into months. By the time things started to slow down, it was almost mid-year. I awoke one day to find that overnight I went from looking as if I was not pregnant, to quite obviously being pregnant. I sat up in bed just staring at my belly. I could not believe how fast it was going. It seemed like just yesterday the Goddess was telling us that we would have a daughter before the end of the year. As I was sitting there thinking about all of that, I felt the first flutters from my little girl. It surprised me so much I yelped, which woke Michael.

"What is wrong My Love?" He asked sleepily.

"I felt the baby move." I said sounding a little breathless.

"Are you serious? I thought it was too early." He said surprised.

"It was not like a kick. It was just a flutter, but it surprised me. That is why I yelped." I explained. He smiled at me before kissing my belly and talking to the baby.

"Good morning little princess. Daddy loves you." He said as he put his hands on my belly. Right after he finished talking, I felt another flutter, and it seemed he felt it too. He kissed my belly again before sitting up and kissing me. We spent the rest of the morning sitting in each other's arms.

We did not move until about midday when Lysandra knocked on the door.

"Come in." I called. She walked in and immediately I knew something was wrong. Lysandra was shaking and she looked as if she had just seen a ghost. I jumped up and went to her. I put my arm around her and lead her to a chair.

"What is wrong Lysa? What happened?" I asked, scared of what her answer would be.

"It was horrible. Stasia I have never seen anything like that before." She said sounding just as scared as she looked.

"What do you mean? Seen what?" I asked getting more worried. "I am so sorry. There was nothing I could do. She was already gone by the time I found her."

"Who? Lysandra who was gone? Who did you find?" I asked thinking I already knew her answer.

"Your mother." I hit the floor. As soon as the words came out of her mouth, my heart stopped and I couldn't breathe. It was like Father all over again.

Michael was at my side in an instant. He pulled me into his arms and I started crying. I could not hold back. He knew there was no calming me right now, so he stepped in.

"Lysandra, where is she? Have you told anyone else?" He asked her gently.

"She is in her room. No one else knows. I came straight here. It is a terrible sight. She did not go gently. She was murdered." Lysandra answered through her tears.

"Michael go find Catalina and bring her here. Lysa can you go make sure no one goes near my mother's room until I am there?" I said calmly, realizing that this meant I am now the Queen and I have to deal with this.

"Of course Stasia." Lysa said before hugging me and leaving to do what I asked. Michael gave me a kiss before leaving too.

Michael was fast. He did not leave me alone for long. Before I had time to start thinking, he was back with Catalina right behind him. She took one look at my face and dropped into the chair that Lysa had just vacated.

"What is wrong Stasia?" She asked, and I could tell she was scared to hear my answer just like I was scared to hear Lysa's.

"Lysa just came to see me. She found Mother murdered in her bed." I said trying to be gentle. "No. It is not possible." Lina cried.

"I have not seen her yet. I wanted to tell you first and see if you would go with me." Lina jumped up and headed for the door with Michael and I right on her heels.

As we headed to Mother's room, I sent a servant to fetch the guards. We got there first and I took Catalina's hand as I opened the door. We both froze in the doorway. There was blood everywhere, on the floor, the walls, the ceiling, and covering the bed. Our mother lay in the middle of the bed. Her eyes were closed and her throat was slashed. It looked as if she had been killed in her sleep.

Once the shock passed, I walked up to my mother. Michael tried stopping me but I pushed his hand away. I had to do it. I had to see her close up. I could not believe that someone had killed my mother in her sleep. She had been a beloved queen. All of her people were devoted to her from the moment she took the throne. I could not think of one person that had ever had an issue with my mother. It just did not make any sense.

The guards arrived and were all shocked by the sight in front of them. They were not expecting to see their queen slain in her bed with blood everywhere. Mother's head guard walked up to me.

"Your Highness, do you know what happened here?" He asked me gently.

"No. All I know is what we all see. Lysandra found her earlier and came straight to me. I had Michael find Catalina and then we came here to see for ourselves. It appears she was killed in her sleep, so at least our queen did not suffer, but it is quite obvious she was murdered. By who I have no clue." I answered trying to sound like a strong queen and not a young woman dying on the inside.

"Okay. The men and I will clean up in here and prepare your mother's body for her funeral. After the funeral, I will question the staff. If that is alright with you Your Highness." He said going into full business mode.

"Of course. Thank you, Tomas. If you need me, I will be

in the Throne Room." I said before leaving and dragging Catalina with me.

Once I was in the Throne Room, I sent servants to gather the entire palace staff, servants, cooks, guards, etc. When they arrived, I was seated on my mother's throne. That sight alone told them what had happened. Once everyone was in, I stood up and addressed them.

"I called you all here to inform you all that my mother was killed in her sleep last night. After her funeral tonight, her Guard will question each and every one of you. If you have any information about my mother's death, you must tell them. If you do not tell them and you are found withholding information, you will be arrested on the spot. That being said, I need the courtyard prepared for The Queen's funeral, the Throne Room prepared for the Ascension Ceremony, and a feast prepared to honor my mother's life and reign. The funeral will take place just before dusk with the Ascension Ceremony to follow. The feast will be held directly after that. Everyone is dismissed to fulfill these tasks, except for my guards and those of you who served my father." I paused to let the others leave. Once it was just the guards left in front of me, I sat down on my new throne.

"Gentlemen, I need you to go out and inform the people of what has happened. My guards will take the areas closest to the palace and those of you from my father's guard will take the outlands. I also need a couple of you to travel to the temple and inform them. We need one of the priestesses to come back with you for the Ascension Ceremony tonight. Please make your journeys as quick as possible and as safe as possible. Remember, we have a killer on the loose with no information as to their identity. So keep your eyes open for anything suspicious while you are out and about. If you see anyone suspicious arrest them on the spot. If you hear anything, follow the lead. Tomorrow morning, I will hold a meeting in here. I want every guard in attendance, no matter who's guard they are in. Thank you. You are dismissed."

Catalina, Michael, and I sat in the Throne Room in silence for a few minutes. None of us knew what to say. In the last few months, we have gone through my return after a three-year disappearance, our father's death at the hand of a man I thought my friend, me becoming pregnant to balance out my father's death, and now our mother has been killed in her bed with no clue as to who did it. Michael and I thought we had a few more months before we would ascend to the throne. We thought it would be a happy occasion, marking our daughter's birth. Instead it will be a sad tearful occasion, marking the untimely demise of my predecessor. I knew we were all thinking the same thing. Why do these things keep happening? First, I was taken from this kingdom for three years with no clue as to how it happened or why, then father was mistakenly killed and now mother was brutally murdered.

Before any of us gathered our thoughts enough to speak,

the door flew open. Damyen walked in and all but ran up to Catalina. He pulled her into his arms.

"I am so sorry Love." He whispered to her as she started crying into his shoulder. He turned to me and said

"I am so sorry Your Highness. I have been away from the palace, visiting my mother who is ill. I just returned and heard the other guards talking about what happened. Is there anything I can do?"

"Thank you Damyen. You are doing exactly what you should be. Stay with Lina while she grieves. She will need you. After we have dealt with everything we need to in the next few days, I will be changing the law so you two can marry." I said sounding more like the queen I now was. He smiled and nodded before leading Catalina out of the Throne Room, leaving Michael and I alone for the first time since I saw my mother's body.

Michael sat down on my father's throne, which was now his. He took my hand in his and pulled me close so he could kiss me. I laid my head on his shoulder and tried to relax. If I did not I would break down, and the Throne Room was not the place for the new queen to have an emotional breakdown. I needed to hold it together until after the feast, when we retired to our room and it was just me and Michael. I had to be strong for my sister and my kingdom. Though quite frankly, I was getting tired of having to be strong for everyone. I am the baby of the family, yet I have to be the one who holds it together no matter what. I should be the one hiding in my room, crying my eyes out into my love's shoulder, but I do not have that luxury.

I was surprised that no one came into the Throne Room to see us. We sat in there alone for over an hour after Catalina and Damyen left. Then all of a sudden the doors flew open and in walked my head guard with a couple priestesses right behind him. I sat up straight and forced a smile for them. I had not expected the priestesses until after the funeral.

"Samuel, you work quick. Thank you." I greeted him.

"Of course Your Highness. This was a matter of great importance." He said before bowing and stepping outside the door.

"Thank you for coming so quickly ladies." I greeted the priestesses.

"Your welcome Your Highness. As soon as your guard appeared at the temple, we knew something was wrong. Your mother's death is a great loss for this kingdom and its people. Please accept our condolences and the knowledge that your mother now sits with the Great Goddess watching over us all as she had when she sat on that throne." Lady Demetrya said respectfully but with the power that all of the goddess's priestesses carried with them.

"Thank you. That does give me great comfort in this terrible time. I will feel more comfortable once we catch her murderer. The guards still have no leads." I told them sadly.

"I may be of some help in that matter Your Highness. If you will allow, I can meditate in the room in which she was killed and I may be able to pick up some readings with my Goddess Gift." Lady Kaytyah spoke up.

"That would be greatly appreciated. I will have my handmaiden show you to my mother's room. The guards should have it cleaned up by now." I said feeling a little better about the situation. As if she knew I was talking about her, Lysandra walked into the Throne Room at that moment.

"Ah wonderful. Lysandra could you show Lady Kaytyah to my mother's room please? And make sure she has whatever she needs to complete her task." I asked Lysa when she got up to me.

"Of course Your Highness. Please follow me M'Lady." Lysa said before turning around and heading back out of the room.

Michael and I spent the next few hours with Lady Demetrya. We went over how the Ascension Ceremony would go. She also helped me to prepare for Mother's funeral, since the funeral of the previous monarch is a little different than the funeral of her husband. Michael surprised me by asking Lady Demetrya to do a blessing on our baby before she heads back to the temple. She was more than happy to oblige his request and we planned it for sunrise the following morning.

My mother's funeral went a lot more smoothly than I expected. Everyone I could see was in tears, even the guards. I spoke of my mother's life and her reign. I spoke of her love for her people and her family. I also gave the people as many details about her death as I could before handing it over to Lady Demetrya, who then did a prayer for my mother's soul. She prayed that her soul finds peace within the Goddess's arms despite her tragic and untimely death. She prayed that her murderer be found quickly and without problems. She also prayed that the Goddess bless not only the kingdom in general during this difficult time, but my family as well and that the Goddess protects the rest of the royal family from further tragedy and heartbreak. Then she dismissed everyone to the Throne Room.

Once everyone was in the Throne Room, Lady Demetrya started the Ascension Ceremony. She read us the oaths and Michael and I swore our lives on them. Then she called on the Goddess to bless us as the new King and Queen. Much to everyone's surprise (even Lady Demetrya) the Goddess appeared in front of us much like she had at Marcus's execution. She smiled out at the people before turning to Michael and I.

"I do not usually appear in form at these ceremonies, but due to all the tragedy and heartbreak that lead to this moment, I felt it necessary. Anastasia and Michael you two have been destined since birth for greatness. The extent of this greatness you know not. I am here to start you off on the right path as King and Queen of my children. From this day until your deaths, you will rule this kingdom and these people before you. They will look to you for guidance and leadership. They will grow strong from the strength inside of both of you. The two of you will do things no other rulers have done. You will have to deal with things none before you have had to deal with. There will be more trying times ahead of you, and at times it may seem easier to give up, but I am here to tell you that if you keep to the path I set you on, you will come out stronger than you ever imagined, as will your kingdom and your children. You will go forth from this day, knowing that I am with you always. Have you need of guidance all you must do is ask for it. On the day of your daughter's birth, an ancient power will awaken in both of you. Use this power for the good of your kingdom and you and yours will be rewarded with happiness and prosperity. I leave you tonight with my blessing and my love. Go forth from this day with peace and serenity in your hearts my beloved children." When she finished her speech, she disappeared just as quickly as she had appeared. Without missing a beat, Lady Demetrya proclaimed us King and Queen, and placed our new crowns atop our heads.

We all went into the banquet hall for the feast in memory of my mother. This feast lasted all night. There was more food than I had ever seen at any other feast in my life. The desserts were piled high on tables ready for the taking whenever someone wanted something. Some muses had traveled down from the temple and were singing, dancing, and playing music. The servants had even hung up paintings of my mother from throughout her life.

About two hours into the feast, I was ready to fall asleep in my seat. Thankfully Michael noticed this. He stood up and gave a short speech thanking everyone for coming and telling them they were welcome to stay and enjoy themselves as long as they wished. Then he helped me up and lead me back to our room.

Once the door closed behind us, I collapsed on to the bed. Michael tried to catch me but was just a little bit too slow. I do not think the baby liked the jostling because she chose that moment to start moving around (for the first time since this morning). I brought my hands up to my belly to feel her movements. I was still amazed at all of it. Michael watched me quietly for a moment, before pulling me into his arms and placing his hands on my belly as well.

"Have you decided what you would like to name her, my love?" He asked, his voice soft and sweet.

"I have a few ideas, but want your input as well. She is your daughter too." I said sounding very tired.

"What are your ideas?" He asked curiously.

"I was thinking either Haven or Adelaide." I told him after a moment of thinking.

"I like those. How should we decide?" He asked me as I started drifting to sleep.

"We shall decide when we see her for the first time." I managed to say before finally slipping into the abyss of sleep.

Chapter Six

Sunrise came much to quickly for me. Lysandra knocked on the door to wake us up for the blessing. We got up and got dressed before heading out to the gardens. Lady Demetrya was waiting for us by my rose bush. Lady Kaytyah and the muses were with her as well. They all curtsied to us as we approached.

"Good morning ladies." I greeted them with a smile.

"Good morning Your Majesties." They said in unison. Lady Demetrya did not waste any time. She got us started on the blessing ritual, which was no small ritual like we had expected. She had put together parts for her and Lady Kaytyah as well as all the muses. If everything they prayed for in the ritual came true for our daughter, then she would not only be a princess of grace and beauty but also of many talents in the arts and skilled in the magikal arts as well.

By the time we were done most of the castle was awake. Lysandra came to find us because I was almost late for my meeting with the guards. Michael and I said goodbye to the priestesses and the muses and then headed to the Throne Room. Half of the guards were already there waiting. We took a seat on our thrones as we waited for the others to arrive. Ten minutes later every guard was standing in front of us. I had them separate into groups based on who's guard they had been in (mine, Catalina's, Mother's, or Father's). Once everyone was separated and I could see how many were in each guard, I stood up and started to address them.

"Thank you for meeting with us this morning. I wanted to call this meeting so we could reassign those of you who had been guarding my parents and to make sure that the separate guards were even. Those of you who were assigned to my father will now be assigned to Michael. Those of you who were assigned to my mother will be split between me, my sister, and Michael until our daughter is born. Then you will be assigned to her guard detail. I would also like it if the Head Guards would search for more men of proper age and ability to join the Royal Guards. With all of the tragedy that has befallen my family lately, I do not want to take any chances, especially with my daughter on the way. If anyone has any questions, ask them now. Otherwise you all are dismissed, except for Tomas." Nobody seemed to have any questions, so they all filed out of the room and went to where ever their stations were.

Once everyone was gone, Tomas walked up to us. He looked as if he had not slept last night, which knowing how he works, wouldn't surprise me.

"Tomas have you gotten any information about my mother's murder since we last spoke?" I asked him trying to be as much of a queen in this moment as I could, but it was still difficult talking about my mother being dead.

"I have questioned each of the servants and most of the guards. They all had no knowledge of anything suspicious happening that night. No one saw anyone come or go from your mother's room. No one heard anything either, but that does not surprise me. She was killed in her sleep so she would not have made any noise. I have some more guards to question today as well as the rest of the staff. As soon as I find out anything, I will let you know." He said formally but there was sadness hidden in his voice.

"The guards that went out yesterday, did they see or hear anything?" I asked, praying that we had some information.

"All they reported was that most of the people had already been talking about the queen having died. They did not know how she died but there had been rumors that she had before the guards had even gone out. It makes me suspicious that the person who killed her was the one who started spreading the rumors, but that still does not get us any closer to finding out who it was."

"Alright. Thank you, Tomas. Please keep us informed."

"Of course Your Majesty." He bowed to us and then left.

The next few hours dragged on. Michael and I had to sit through multiple meetings. The farmers came in to report what seemed like the start of a drought out in the fields, and the miners came in to report that they had found a new cave where they would be mining more precious gems than they had ever seen in one area. With every new person that walked into the Throne Room, I prayed that they would be coming to give us some information on my mother's death, but I was disappointed every time.

Finally, it was time for dinner. Michael and I headed into the banquet hall to eat. Catalina was already seated and sipping on some tea. This was the first time I had seen her all day. She looked like the picturesque princess. Not a strand of hair was out of place, and there were no tear stains on her cheeks. Only someone who knew her as well as I did would be able to see the signs of her grief.

When Catalina saw us walk in, she walked over to us and gave me a hug. She had not hugged me like that since she pulled me back through the portal. It was as if she had been worried that she would lose me too. I hugged her back and whispered to her that everything will be alright. We will get through this. She smiled at me before leading us back over to our table.

Dinner was uneventful. We ate our meal and made small talk. Catalina kept asking questions about the baby. She especially wanted to know what her niece's name would be, and she was disappointed when I told her that we hadn't decided yet.

The cooks had made strawberry and crème truffles for dessert. I was extremely excited because we had not had these since my wedding. But that excitement was short lived.

About halfway through my dessert, Tomas came running in. He was extremely out of breath and looked as if he had just been in a fight. When he caught his breath enough to speak, he looked back and forth between me and Catalina.

"We found your mother's killer." He said, his voice sounding very rough.

"What? Who is it? Do you have them in custody?" I asked sounding more like a grieving daughter than a queen.

"She managed to slip away before we were able to get her in custody but my men are pursuing her. None of us have any idea who she is but she said you two will know her. As soon as we have her in custody, I will bring her to you Your Majesty." He explained sounding very pissed that he did not have her yet.

"Thank you, Tomas. When you get her back here, put her straight into a cell. Then come find me and Catalina." I ordered.

"Of course Your Majesty." Tomas left right away to go catch up with his men. "Finally. This nightmare is almost over." I said to no one in particular.

After dessert I headed into my new office. Lysandra was in there still working on switching everything over from my mother's stuff to mine.

"Good evening Stasia." She said with a sad smile.

"Hello Lysa. How are you doing?" I asked.

"I am okay. I have been busy switching everything and getting the nursery cleaned up so it will be ready for when the little princess makes her entrance. What are you doing? I did not think you would be coming in here until your mother's stuff was taken care of."

"I had planned on staying out of here until then, but something needs my attention. I made a promise over eight years ago, and it is about time I fulfilled it." I said surprising her. She did not ask any more questions. She grabbed me a piece of parchment and a pen. Then I sat down at my desk and started drafting up a revision to the marriage law. This revision would allow women who cannot bear children to marry if they find a suitable husband willing to forego having children. Once it was written, I sent Lysa to find Michael. I needed both of our signatures to make the revision an official law. He signed it as soon as he read it. He knew why I was doing this and agreed completely with me. I then gave the revision to the Historian to file it. He would also get the word out to all of the kingdom.

When I was done with everything I needed to do to change the law, I was exhausted. Michael was bringing me back to our room so I could sleep. Right around the corner from our room we were stopped. It was Damyen.

"Your Majesties! Catalina sent me to find you. The guards have returned." He said a little out of breath. His expression told me it was not good news. We followed him back to the Throne Room.

"What is going on? I told Tomas to bring the prisoner straight to the cells." I asked confused.

"There is no need to detain her Your Majesty." Damyen said.

He opened the door and inside the Throne Room was every guard in our employ. They were circled around something in the middle of the Throne Room. When I walked in the guards moved aside for me. Laying on the floor in front of me was a woman a few years younger than me. One look at her face and I knew exactly who she was. I couldn't believe it though. It was impossible. She had died when I was eight years old. Catalina and I had watched her die out in the fields behind the palace.

I heard someone crying near me, and that was when I realized that Catalina had already been there. She was kneeling on the floor a few feet from me, and she was crying into Damyen's shoulder. She had recognized the girl too.

It was all too much for me. I dropped to my knees beside the girl and started crying. Michael had no idea who she was or what was going on but he could take a hint. He dismissed all the guards and then knelt down beside me. He wrapped his arms around me and held me as I cried. Once the tears halted I was able to speak but Michael cut me off.

"My Love, who is this girl?" He asked softly. "Her name was Rhiannon and she was our baby sister." Catalina answered before I had a chance.

"But I thought your parents only had the two of you."

Damyen said just as confused as Michael.

"Rhiannon had died ten years ago. The three of us were out in the fields playing and the next thing we knew, she was dead on the ground. Catalina and I carried her body back to the palace. Mother was a mess when she saw what happened. We had a small funeral for her, just the family. And after the funeral, she was never mentioned again. Mother forbid us to speak of her. We figured it was because it was too painful for her, but now she shows up here after ten years, not as a long-lost sister, but as the woman who killed our mother. I do not understand." I explained to them while trying to make sense of it all in my own head. Catalina came over beside me and looked down at our baby sister's body.

"I want to know what happened to her when we were little. We watched her burn on her funeral pyre." She said to me.

"I would like to know that as well, but it seems we may never know. With her dead, we have no leads on what happened to her and no reasoning behind her killing Mother." I told Catalina.

Catalina and I had another funeral for our baby sister. We did not want to cause a big uproar among the people so it was only family and the palace staff. We sent word out through the kingdom that the queen's murderer had been found dead. It seemed like that would be the end of it all, so we moved on with our lives.

I started working on preparations for the Midyear Festival,

and Catalina started planning her wedding, which was to be the main event at this year's festival. I had never seen Catalina so busy, or so happy. Each day brought us closer to her finally having her happy ending, and she made sure to let everyone know that the tragedy that has befallen our family in the last few months would not hinder her happiness. Our parents would not want us to live our lives always feeling sad and depressed, so we made the most of every day.

When the first day of the Midyear Festival came upon us, Catalina had everything set for her wedding to take place the following night. The outside of the palace was set for the festival and for our people to arrive, and the inside was set for a royal wedding. The palace staff was running around like crazed chickens trying to make sure everything was perfcct, though I already saw it as perfect.

Right after breakfast, I decided to take a stroll through the festival area as the vendors were setting up their stalls. Every one of them paused to greet me, and most offered me a free sample of their wares. The only one I was not able to politely turn down was a pastry from one of the bakers stalls. As soon as I smelled it, the baby started doing somersaults in my belly and would not stop until I ate the pastry. After I finished it, I could not stop laughing. I couldn't believe that my little princess was controlling me so much already and she wasn't even born yet.

The festival started out just as it was supposed to. I opened it with a blessing and then the public were allowed in to check out all the vendors and the different entertainment tents. Michael and I had a blast socializing with all of our people. A few of the vendors even gave us gifts for the baby. By the time the sun set, not only was I exhausted but I was full of all the delicious foods and pastries we had tried from all the vendors and our arms were full of baby gifts and new jewels for me.

The next day was a little busier. I could not spend the day just doing whatever. I had to make sure everything was set for my sister's wedding that night. I ran around all morning making sure everything was decorated correctly and making sure the kitchen had everything they needed for the feast. Most of what I was doing I could have and probably should have left to Lysandra and Catalina's handmaiden, but this wedding was my big success. It marked the moment when I was able to fulfill my promise to Lina, so I wanted everything perfect. I ended up spending the afternoon with Lina in her dressing chambers. She was a nervous wreck. I tried to calm her by getting her to soak in a lavender infused bath. It worked a little bit.

About an hour away from the wedding Shealah finally arrived with Lina's wedding dress. It was almost as beautiful as mine. It was a similar style but had no lace. Lina was not a girl for lace. Instead it had gorgeous bead work all over the skirt and the corset was decorated with the most amazing stitching I had ever seen. It was obvious Shealah tried to put in just as much effort on this gown as she did on mine. She had been working on it from the day that I changed the law allowing Lina to marry. We got Lina dressed and I did her hair. Lysandra brought in some jewelry for her from my collection (mine was much bigger than Lina's).

By the time we were finished getting her ready, there were only five minutes until she was supposed to walk down the aisle. We all walked down to the Throne Room together, before leaving Lina outside the doors while we went to find our places. As I walked in, Damyen was standing up front looking just as nervous as Lina had earlier. I smiled at him and motioned for him to breath. He smiled back and took a couple deep breaths. Then the doors opened and revealed to him his beautiful bride.

Lina looked like a goddess. She stood in the doorway for a moment staring at Damyen. She never thought she was going to get to this point, even after I made her that promise, and here she was, about to walk down the aisle. She put a smile on her face and started walking. With each step the smile got more and more genuine, and the smile on Damyen's face grew and grew. I felt so good knowing that I had been the one to bring these two to this point of happiness.

The ceremony went much the same way as mine. When the priestess declared them husband and wife, Damyen kissed Lina and I could see the tears streaming down her cheeks. For the first time in months (maybe even years) Lina was crying tears of joy.

The feast was beautiful. The banquet hall had been decorated with violets and golden candles. The cooks prepared all of Lina's favorite foods and just about every dessert item in existence. We had enough food to feed our family for three years plus. It was a good thing that royal weddings were public affairs, or most of the food would have gone to waste. A couple muses had come down from the temple for the festival and they were dancing in honor of Lina and Damyen's love. A few of their dance routines were prayers, and I swear one of them was a prayer for children (but I could be wrong). Everyone knew that Lina could not have children and I did not think the Goddess would change that now, though my sister would make a wonderful mother.

I awoke the next day to tragedy. The entire festival yard had been burned to the ground. Nobody had been hurt but all the vendors had lost their products they had brought to sell. Nothing like this had ever happened in the history of the festival. And to make it worse, the guards had no leads as to who had done it.

Michael and I walked through the remains of the festival yard. Everything was scorched or completely burned to ash. I looked in every stall, or what were stalls. Not even the smallest scrap of paper had escaped the flames...or so I thought.

In the last stall, which had been the bakers stall who I had visited during the festival setup, things were different. The stall itself was burned along with everything on the counter. But in the back, where she kept her stock, everything was fine. Not a scorch mark to be found. I could smell the scent of the pastries mixing with the smell of burning wood.

I sent Samuel to find the baker and anyone she had helping her at her stall. The stall owner looked scared and upset, and her worker looked like she had better things to do. My suspicion automatically fell on the worker.

"Your Majesty, you wanted to see us?" The stall owner said once they were in front of me.

"Yes I did. What is your name?" I asked her.

"My name is Chelsey and this is my sister in law's daughter Maggie. She has been helping me in the shop and was helping me here yesterday." The stall owner replied.

"Chelsey, I have been looking over the festival yard, or what remains of it, along with my guards. Every stall and its contents are completely destroyed except for yours. Your stall was burnt but your supply in the back was untouched. I thought it kind of odd that of all the stalls yours was the only one not completely destroyed." I informed her. She looked shocked. She had no idea her stuff was not destroyed. Her niece however did not seem that surprised, so I turned my attention to her.

"Maggie, do you like working with your aunt?" I asked her all of a sudden. My question definitely caught her off guard.

"It is not bad work. I assume I could have it worse." She replied matter of factly.

"Would you like to keep working with her?" I asked, once again throwing her off guard.

"Yes. That was my plan, at least until I marry." She answered after a moment of hesitation. Chelsey was watching our conversation trying to figure out where it was going.

"Then you need to tell me what you know about this fire, right now, or one of my guards over there will be putting you in a cell." I said finally getting to the point. Chelsey was shocked, but Maggie was not. She had not realized until that point that I suspected her at all.

"I do not know anything Your Majesty." She said trying to play dumb, but I was not a stupid woman.

"Okay then. Samuel!" I called. He started walking towards us, and Maggie's eyes almost jumped out of her head.

"Okay okay. I am sorry Your Majesty. She said if I told anyone, she would kill my family. I have seen the things she does, and she is not one you want to cross." Maggie said as she started crying.

"Who is she?" I asked.

"Her name is Rhiannon."

"How do you know her?" I asked, trying to keep my shock hidden.

"We met when we were young. We used to play together out in the woods. She disappeared for a few years but she returned a couple years ago. When she returned, she was different. There was some kind of power that radiated from her, and she seemed like she had a mission to complete. It was like nothing mattered to her except that mission. Then a few months ago, about the time you returned to the kingdom, she changed again. The power was still there, but she seemed as if she had completed her mission, whatever it was. She spent more time with me." Maggie explained, sounding extremely scared to be saying it out loud.

"Did she set the fire last night?" I asked, not really wanting to know the answer because it would create more questions, like how did she survive her funeral pyre that Lina and I had for her.

"Yes Your Majesty." Maggie said sounding defeated.

"Where can I find her?"

The next few hours were spent in deep conversation with my guards. Maggie gave me all the information I needed. We set up a plan to find Rhiannon and capture her. Michael was not too keen on the plan though.

"Ana you cannot go with the guards. It is too dangerous. We have no idea how she survived two funeral pyres. Its not safe for you or the baby." He begged as I was getting ready to leave.

"Michael if I do not do it who will?"

It was at that moment that Catalina arrived.

"I will. I want to figure this out just as much as you do Stasia and I am not as important to the kingdom as you are. If something happens to you, our kingdom will lose its Queen and its heiress. So you stay here with Michael and Damyen, and I will go with the guards."

"But if something happens to you, I will never be able to forgive myself." I argued, though I knew it was useless. She was right, as always.

The next few hours were torture. We had no way to communicate with the guards after they left the palace, which left me sitting around trying not to go insane with worry. Michael, Damyen, and Lysandra tried to keep me occupied but it only worked for a short while. No matter how many baby preparations Lysa came up with, or how many people Michael and Damyen brought to me for help, I could not keep from thinking about my men who I just sent into danger, or my big sister who is risking her life in my place.

Almost four hours after everyone headed out, a young guard walked into the Throne Room. Samuel sent him as a messenger to inform me of what has happened so far. It turns out that Rhiannon's hideout was not as well protected as Maggie had thought. My men broke in in a matter of minutes. They fought some guards that Rhiannon had acquired, and walked away with no casualties of our own. All of her men were dead though. When the messenger had been sent back to us, Samuel was getting ready to lead Catalina into the center of the hideout, where Rhiannon would be. After he finished relaying his message, he headed back out to help.

Hearing from Samuel both calmed some of my worry and brought out new worry. I was happy to hear that none of my men had been killed or even hurt in the initial battle. Our guards were hard to replace, and I have been close to many of them for years. But now I was worrying even more about Catalina. I had no clue what she was doing or dealing with, and all I wanted to do was swoop in and save her from whatever it was.

Thankfully, my little princess decided it was time to wake up and play. Feeling her move in my belly helped to calm some of my fears and worries. It also reminded me of why I was doing all of this. I did not want to bring my little girl into a world where she had to watch her back for some evil aunt we had all thought dead years ago. I wanted her to know the happiness and the security that Catalina and I grew up with. This was a peaceful kingdom, and I would be damned if it did not go back to being that way.

A little while later I was sitting in the garden with Lysandra. We were just chatting about life. It was as if nothing was going on. Just two friends hanging out, but then everyone returned. The guards walked up the path from the main gates. I did not see Catalina anywhere. I ran to Samuel calling out for Catalina as I went. Samuel smiled at me...which told me she was not hurt.

"Your sister needs to talk to you Your Majesty. She went around back and should be in your office now." Samuel said with a bow. Without a word I ran inside to my office.

Catalina stood in the center of my office pacing back and forth. At first I thought she was alone, but then I stepped around my desk to sit down and saw Rhiannon sitting across from me. I froze. I had no clue what to do or what to say. I had figured if I saw her alive again it would be in chains seeing how she did murder my mother and burned down our festival, but here she was sitting across from me as if we were just two people in a meeting.

Catalina came around to me and put her hand on my shoulder, trying to get me to calm down and sit. I looked at her briefly, long enough to see her nod at me. Sitting down, I asked to both of them, "What is going on?"

"Stasia you have to listen to what she has to say. It is going to sound very bizarre at first but it will make sense afterwards. Please just listen to her." Catalina said in a pleading tone.

"How did you get the guards to allow her to come here without chains?" I asked Catalina.

"Samuel was with me when she explained her story to me. He heard everything I did and we both came to the agreement that you needed to hear her out." Lina answered before Rhiannon jumped in.

"If you feel more comfortable having this conversation with me in a cell, then that is fine, as long as you hear me out." Rhiannon said softly but powerfully. I took a deep breath before turning to look at my baby sister.

"Rhiannon, the last time we spoke I was eight years old and I had watched you die. The last time I saw you, you were lying dead on the floor in front of my throne and had just killed our mother the night before. I will give you five minutes to explain everything to me before I call Samuel to lock you up." I said sounding very much like the queen I was supposed to be in this situation.

Rhiannon nodded before starting her story.

"Mother never allowed you guys to speak of me after I died as a kid and no one outside the castle knew of my existence. This was not because of a grieving mother who could not bear the heartache over her dead child. It was because the mother could not bear to think anymore of how that child had come to be. Yes, I was the Queen's daughter, but I was not the King's. Mother had gone off to visit the temple for some reason and on her way home she was attacked. Her attackers had no idea who she was, otherwise, they would have not done it, but during the attack she was not just robbed. Mother had been raped and nine months later, I was born. Your father convinced her that everything would be alright. That they could pass me off as his, but as I got older that became more and more difficult. It turns out my father was not just some common criminal. He had magical abilities that were passed on to me. As I got older, these abilities started coming out at the worst times. They started hiding me from the public. Eventually everyone outside the palace had forgotten me and even the staff that did not deal directly with me, had started to forget too. Then that day when we were all playing out in the field, I was running after you guys and all of a sudden, I could feel the power in me building until the next thing I knew I was waking up in a cave. After you guys had held my funeral, my father had found my body and brought me back to the caves in which he and his men lived. When I awoke, he explained everything to me. I was not some weird princess meant to be kept hidden. I was the first of his kind to be born in over three centuries."

"Wait a second. What do you mean his kind?" I jumped in cutting her off before she could continue. She smiled. She had been hoping I would catch that.

"My father is not human, and neither am I." She said.

"What? If you are not human, then what are you?" I asked, starting to get confused and rather irritated.

"We are of a magical race that is able to wield magical abilities and after the age of 15 we do not age. My father is their leader." She explained as if this was not the most bizarre thing I had ever heard.

"You realize how ridiculous that sounds?" I asked.

"Stasia, think about it. How else would she have survived two funeral pyres?" Catalina jumped in.

"Right that reminds me. You did not explain your deaths, and how they did not truly kill you." I said turning back to Rhiannon.

"My first death was when my magic fully awoke. When one of us reaches a certain level of magical use, our body shuts down for a while to adjust. My second death was my body hitting full maturity for my kind. It shut down to complete the change. I will not age another day past the day your guards brought my body to you." She answered matter of factly.

"Okay so what about Mother? You killed her. How are you going to try to talk yourself out of that one." I demanded, my anger starting to surpass my confusion.

"I did not kill her. I can show you who did, but you won't like the answer. Yes, I was in the room when she died, but I did not kill her. I confronted her. I figured since your father was gone, it would be easier to talk to her, but I was wrong. She freaked out when she saw me. She thought she was seeing a ghost and refused to listen when I told her I was not dead, that I was alive and had been all these years."

"What do you mean you can show me who killed her?" I interrupted.

"It is one of my abilities. I can show other things I have witnessed in the past." Rhiannon said proudly.

She took my hands in hers and said to do as she says. I figured I would humor her for a moment, so when she told me to stay quiet and close my eyes, I listened. A few moments later, it was as if I were transported to my mother's room, yet I could still feel my chair underneath me and Rhiannon's hands in mine.

My mother was lying in her bed asleep. All of a sudden, the door opened and in walked Rhiannon. She woke my mother up, and instinctively Mother jumped up and screamed when she saw she was being woken up by her dead daughter. Rhiannon tried to soothe her and explain that she was not dead, and that Mother was in no danger. Rhiannon just wanted to talk, but Mother would hear none of it. She kept trying to get away and to call for the guards. Rhiannon told Mother that they would not come, because she put a charm on the room so no noise would leave it. This only made Mother more nervous. As Rhiannon was trying to think of how to fix the situation, Mother grabbed a knife. Rhiannon thought it was meant for her and jumped back. As she backed away, Mother brought the knife across her throat and then put it through her own heart. I watched as my mother took her own life to get away from the daughter she never wanted.

Back in the present I pulled my hands out of Rhiannon's and buried my face in them. The tears started streaming down my face. I could not speak or even think. Even when the baby started moving, I could not pull myself out of it. Catalina and Rhiannon tried everything, but nothing worked. Lina sent for Michael. When he arrived, he was first surprised to see Rhiannon, and then surprised to see me in that state.

"What is going on?" He demanded of Catalina.

"We finally learned the truth." She answered.

"What does that mean?" he asked completely confused.

"It means they learned all the secrets their parents have been keeping from them for 15 years. Now stop fussing around talking to us. Your wife needs you." Rhiannon spit at him. Michael glowered at her but did not say another word. He came right over to me and picked me up. He carried me back to our bedroom and laid me on the bed.

I woke up some time later. I had no idea how long I had been asleep, but I was starving. I got up and headed down to the dining hall. I could smell the delicious fragrance of breakfast cooking and realized I had slept all night. The servants rushed off to get me food and Lysandra went to find Michael and Catalina. Michael arrived first. He pulled me into his arms and kissed me.

"I am so sorry my love." He whispered in my ear. "Did they tell you what they told me?" I asked curiously.

"Yes, and Rhiannon showed me too. I wanted to know exactly what put you in that state you were in last night. I cannot believe that your mother would do that. Not after having just gotten you back and having lost your father." He said sadly.

"Honestly I think that is exactly why she did it. It was too much for her and she knew if she left that room she was going to have to put on a strong face and keep it together for the sake of the kingdom. I do not think she had it in her to deal with it all anymore." I said as the realization hit me.

"So she left the mess for you to deal with?" Michael asked.

"Mother knew the kingdom would be in good hands with Stasia on the throne." Catalina said as she joined us.

"Where is Rhiannon?" I asked.

"She is in my chambers for now. Damyen is with her. Until I spoke with you I did not want to make a big scene but I did not want her to be alone." Catalina informed me.

"Can you have Damyen bring her here? And Michael can you fetch Lysandra and Shealah for me please?" I asked, trying to push my emotions aside and be the queen I needed to be.

A few minutes later Damyen walked in with Rhiannon on his heels. She wore a hooded cloak, which I thought was a great idea, because if people started seeing her before I had set my plans in motion, there would be an uproar of confusion. Damyen gave me a quick hug before going to sit by Catalina, and Rhiannon sat beside me. A servant brought both of them a plate of food. Rhiannon did not touch hers, but turned to me expectantly.

"We did not get to my final question last night." I said calmly.

"What is it?" She asked curiously.

"What happened with the festival yard?" I asked, sounding as if I had asked her what the weather outside was.

"Oh right. I had sent one of my men to check on things here and he had a run in with a girl from his past. An argument started and next thing he knew, he had set the stalls nearest to him on fire. Everything he tried to put the fire out, made it grow larger, so he got out of there and came home."

"So why was the stall your friend Maggie worked at the only one not completely destroyed?"

"I showed her a few small spells that anyone could do back when we were young and the protection charm was always her favorite."

At that moment, Michael walked in with Lysandra and Shealah behind him. It had been a long time since I had seen Shealah. She looked a lot happier than the last time we saw each other.

"Thank you for coming so quickly Shealah." I said, trying to keep my voice neutral. She smiled sweetly and said

"Of course Your Majesty. What is it you need of me?" "I need you to try and find some gowns for Rhiannon here. Some everyday ones and a party dress for tonight." I informed her, surprising just about everyone in our little group.

"Of course Your Majesty. Rhiannon I can take you to my

shoppe and we can find everything you need." Shealah said.

"Before you ladies leave, I need to finish. Lysandra I need you to get the word out that the festival's ball will still take place tonight and that we will have a special guest of honor. Do not let out who the guest is and make sure the staff gets the palace ready quickly. We will also need another throne added to the Throne Room. Michael, can you send for Samuel to accompany Rhiannon to Shealah's shoppe?"

Lysandra went off to get started on the tasks I had assigned her and Michael went off to find Samuel. That left me with two very confused sisters, a brother in law and a mistress. I smiled and laughed at the looks of complete confusion on their faces.

"Stasia what is going on?" Catalina finally asked, when it became apparent that I was not going to explain myself without some prompting.

"I am giving Rhiannon what she should have been given at birth. Despite the situation that brought her into existence, she is a daughter of the previous queen, which means she is a princess of this kingdom and as its current queen, I have the right to bestow upon her the title and privileges of her birthright. We will make her existence known tonight at the ball, where she will be crowned as our truly long lost princess and she will take her place on the throne next to us." I finally explained, shocking everyone around me. Shealah, who had no idea who Rhiannon was until that moment, was stunned speechless. Damyen looked to Catalina to see her reaction.

Catalina was staring at me as if she did not recognize me, and Rhiannon was starting to tear up. She threw her arms around me and hugged me tight.

"Thank you Stasia!" Rhiannon said softly as she wiped her face.

"What about your other family Rhiannon?" Catalina asked.

"I have never completely felt comfortable there. Yes I am an important person to them but the only place I have ever felt at home was with the two of you. All I wanted when I came here and talked to Mother was answers and some acceptance." Rhiannon said a little uncomfortably.

A couple hours before the Ball was set to begin, I was walking through the palace making sure everything was all set. I knew Lysandra would make sure my every command was fulfilled, but I liked supervising party preparations myself. The Ballroom was decorated perfectly, and the guards had brought in a new throne. The banquet hall was set with enough places for the entire kingdom, and I could smell the feast cooking from the kitchens down the hall. Everything was perfect.

In my dressing room, Rhiannon was getting ready with Catalina, Lysandra, and Shealah. I smiled as I looked over my little sister. She looked like the princess she was born to be...well almost.

"Rhiannon, I had this made for myself when I came home but never got the chance to wear it before becoming queen.

I thought it would look perfect on you." I said as I held up a beautiful silver tiara with rubies encrusted in it. Rhiannon actually squealed in delight when she saw it. Luckily Lysandra had planned for a tiara. She had done Rhiannon's hair perfectly to fit around the tiara.

"There. Now you look like a princess." I said smiling. She hugged me tightly, and had a huge smile on her face.

I walked into the ballroom and was surprised to see how packed it was. The Festival Ball was always a big event, but this was the biggest I had ever seen. It seemed like every citizen of my kingdom was in this room. My little tease about a surprise guest of honor must have gotten everyone's attention.

I went up to my throne and called everyone's attention.

"Thank you all for coming tonight. I know this festival has not been what we expected. I wanted to apologize for the fire in the festival yard. It was started by accident. Every vendor who lost their wares in the fire may come to me tomorrow and I will pay you for your losses. I also want to thank everyone who came out to my sister's wedding the other night. Princess Catalina was beyond overjoyed to see everyone. Now to get to the part you have all been waiting for. Our guest of honor tonight is someone I thought gone for good years ago, but in the process of trying to find out the truth behind my mother's death, I discovered that I was not this kingdom's only lost princess. My mother had another daughter after I was born. She was hidden from the people because she was not my father's daughter. My mother had been raped and when she gave birth to a child from this rape, my father convinced my mother that it would be okay. They would pass her off as his. But it turned out that that would be impossible, so they hid her from everyone. Even the palace staff did not know of her existence. When I was eight years old, Catalina and I were playing with our baby sister out in the fields and all of a sudden it seemed like she had just dropped dead. After her funeral, Mother forbid us to speak of her. As time went on, we had even managed to forget about her, until a few weeks ago when the guards brought her in as a suspect in my mother's murder. By the time she had gotten here, her body had shut down and we thought she was dead, but one look at her face and Catalina and I knew it was our baby sister. Then in searching for the cause behind the fire yesterday, we discovered our baby sister was alive. Catalina went to take her into custody with the guards. In the process, she learned the truth. A truth that was then shared with me, one I did not want to believe but has since been proven true. My mother was not killed. She took her own life as a result of my baby sister trying to confront her and get answers and some acceptance from a mother who had never wanted her. Mother thought she was being haunted by the ghost of her dead daughter. The only way she could think to save herself from it was to take her life. She knew she would be with the Goddess and with my father, and she knew the kingdom would be in good hands with me on the throne. Now we are here tonight to give my baby sister her birthright. As Queen, I have the ability to grant titles to anyone I see fit, and as a daughter of the previous queen, my baby sister is entitled to the position that Catalina and I grew up with. I would like to introduce you all to my baby sister, Princess Rhiannon."

I spoke to the people with every ounce of power I had. When I finished, the doors to the ballroom opened to reveal Rhiannon standing with Catalina. Rhiannon walked slowly through the crowd, which parted for her. Once she reached me, I hugged her quickly before turning back to the crowd in front of us.

"Please welcome Princess Rhiannon. She may not have been raised here in the kingdom or in the palace, but she is a princess of this kingdom and she will be there for all of you just as Catalina and I have been." I said before leading Rhiannon over to the thrones. I took my seat and she slowly sat on her new throne. We were then joined by Michael and Catalina. Damyen stood slightly behind Catalina's throne.

The ball went on all night without incident. The people danced and ate and mingled with each other. Many of them came up to personally welcome Rhiannon, which made her night. Towards the end, Damyen was called away by a young lord. They had a whispered conversation before he came back and whispered to me.

"It seems your little sister already has an admirer. The Lord Nathan wishes to approach her." He said softly so only I could hear. I smiled before whispering his message to Rhiannon. She looked over at Nathan then nodded to me. Damyen brought Nathan over and introduced him.

"Princess Rhiannon, this is Lord Nathan." Lord Nathan took Rhiannon's hand and kissed it before looking up at her with a soft smile.

"It is nice to meet you Your Highness. I wanted to personally welcome you to the kingdom and ask if you would honor me with a dance." He said sweetly. Rhiannon blushed. "Thank you my lord. I would love to dance." She said before standing up. Rhiannon and Lord Nathan danced the rest of the night away. They were even still dancing when Michael and I went to bed.

Chapter Seven

The next day we were awakened by a very excited Lysandra. She was just about bouncing out of her skin with excitement. I had to force her into a chair to get her to calm down long enough to talk.

"What has gotten you so excited Lysa?" I asked her. "I have lots of news Stasia!" She said and it looked like she was about to jump out of her seat.

"Well get on with it then girl." I urged her impatiently.

"That Lord from the ball last night has come to request your permission to court Princess Rhiannon. Shealah has sent word to you announcing her engagement to James. And I have been approached by a lovely young man as well." The words just about flew out of her mouth. I could not believe it. After all the tragedy and loss we have all gone through since my disappearance, getting all this good news all at once seemed weird, but I went with it. I was excited. My baby sister has found a suitor in less than 24 hours of being named a Princess, and both of my best friends have found suitors as well. How could I not be excited?

Michael woke up then. He looked around and was surprised to see me and Lysandra sitting over by the window.

"What's going on love?" He asked me sleepily.

"Looks like we have some more weddings to plan." I said excited.

"What? Who's?" He asked more awake now.

"Shealah and James have announced their engagement. Lysandra is being courted and Lord Nathan is waiting to ask my permission to court Rhiannon. Of course she still has a little while before she can marry. She hasn't actually turned 15 yet, but her birthday is coming up." I told him and his shock was very evident on his face.

The next few weeks went by slowly. Most of my time was filled with preparing for my daughter's birth as she was due in a month. I also had my usual queenly duties to uphold but my sisters helped with as much as they could. Michael helped Rhiannon adjust to palace life, seeing how he was the only one of us who hadn't completely grown up here. Even Damyen had grown up in the palace, being a royal guard and the son of a royal guard. Lysandra was busy planning her wedding around her regular duties and Shealah had finally set a date for hers.

I was walking through the gardens with Rhiannon discussing plans for her birthday which was a few days before the baby was due. Since it would be her 15th birthday, I was planning on throwing a ball and Lord Nathan could finally propose to her. She was more excited than even Catalina was on her wedding day. After I told her what I wanted for the ball, she went off to talk to the servants and get started planning it. This would be her first time planning a royal ball.

A servant came up to me after Rhiannon left to deliver the invitation from Shealah. I opened it to discover her wedding was the day after Rhiannon's ball. It seemed that week would be full of happiness, Rhiannon's first birthday as a princess, Shealah's wedding, and my daughter's birth, or so I thought.

The morning of Rhiannon's birthday, I was eating breakfast with Michael. Everyone was running around making sure the last-minute preparations for the ball that night were set. It seemed like we would have nothing to do that day, but then a terrified farmer came running. I instantly recognized him. He was the one who had brought my father's body home after Marcus had killed him.

"Your Majesties! I have terrible news!" He said out of breath. You could hear his fear in his voice.

"What is it sir?" I asked, afraid to hear what he would say.

"There is an illness going around. It started last night. People are getting sick and dying from it. It starts with a cough and a fever, but then they start puking blood. Before you know it they are dead."

"What? Where is this happening? How many have died?" Michael asked worried for our people but scared it would spread here and affect his family.

"In the outlands. It has not spread across the fields, yet. When I received word of it, ten people had died. But that was over an hour ago so it could be much more by now." The farmer answered.

"Okay go home. Bring your family inside and keep them there. Make sure everyone washes up and then ties a cloth over their mouth and nose in case it is spread through the air. If you get anymore word from the outlands, send a message straight to me." Michael says, trying to push his fears aside and get to business.

The farmer left to do what he was told. Michael called the guard from outside the door. He sent him to gather all the guards and the handmaidens. I sat by waiting to hear Michael's plan. Once everyone was there, Michael called their attention.

"We have just received word that there is an illness spreading through the outlands. People are getting a cough and a fever and then they start puking blood. This illness is killing everyone who gets it. I need word to get out to the villages to warn them. They need to all stay in their homes. They need to wash and cover their mouths and noses. I also need the handmaidens to help secure and cleanse the castle. All windows are to be closed. Everyone needs to wash, and anything that has come in from outside the castle in the last couple of days, needs to be cleansed. Everyone is dismissed to get to work, except Samuel and Lysandra." Michael informed and ordered everyone at once. When everyone else had left the room, Michael turned to Samuel and Lysandra.

"Lysandra, I need you to take Stasia and help her bathe.

While she is in the bath, close up all the windows in our room and cleanse it. Then bring her there. You two must stay in there until I say otherwise. Samuel, you are to make sure no one goes in there unless you hear an okay from me directly." Michael ordered them. They nodded and started walking towards the door but stopped when they realized I was not following. "What are you going to do?" I asked my husband, just now realizing that he was going to take care of this on his own.

"I am going to inform your sisters of what is going on and try to figure out how to stop this illness from annihilating our kingdom. I cannot do that unless I know you and our daughter are safe." Michael said and he stroked my cheek. "If you want me to hide in my room while you are out risking your life, you do not know me very well." I said stubbornly, knowing it was useless.

"My love, you need to go with Lysa and Samuel. They will protect you. If it makes you feel better I will send Catalina to stay with you once she has bathed." "Fine. But what about Rhiannon?" I asked, giving in.

"She has lived in the mountains near the outlands the majority of her life. She may know something about this illness. Plus she cannot be killed, so I think she is my best ally in fighting whatever this is." Michael said before kissing me. I nodded and left with Lysa.

We went straight to my dressing room. She got to work right away in preparing a bath for me. Once I was in, she went to walk to my bedroom.

"Wait!" I called.

"What is it Stasia?" She asked confused.

"There is no point of you going into my room to cleanse it unless you have washed too. This tub is big enough for my whole family. Take a few minutes to bathe before you go to my room." I told her, trying to sound like I knew what I was talking about. Honestly, I was just scared of being alone right now. Lysa nodded and got into the tub. We both washed up and when we were done, she dressed quickly and ran to my room. While she was cleaning it, I stayed in the dressing room. I found a comfy gown to slip into and then decided since I was going to be stuck in my room without having to deal with the public, I would not dress up like normal. I kept my hair down and wore the minimal amount of jewelry I could personally allow myself. A little while later, Lysandra returned. She was smiling, which made me wonder what was going on.

She lead me out and down the hall to my room. Catalina and Damyen were inside already, and there was a tray of food laid out for us, a long with a few bottles of wine.

"I do not know how long we will be in here, so I wanted to make sure we had enough to get us through for a while." Lysa said when she saw me staring at the food and wine. I laughed before turning to Catalina and Damyen. Lina threw her arms around me.

"Stasia!" She cried.

"It is okay Lina. We are okay. It has not spread across the fields." I said trying to reassure her.

"But that does not mean it will not." Lina said, sounding frightened.

"Michael and Rhiannon will figure something out." I said sounding much surer of myself than I felt. Truthfully, I was just as scared as Catalina. We all sat down and had a glass of wine. All we could do now was wait.

"Michael!"

Rhiannon called as I walked past her in the hall.

"What is it Rhiannon?" I asked, praying she had some good news for me. It had been hours since the farmer had brought us news of the illness, and we were no closer to stopping it than we were then.

"I have contacted my father. He wants to speak with you. He said he may know what the illness is." She said sounding scared and excited.

"Wonderful!" I said as I followed her back to her chambers.

In the middle of her bedroom there was a large mirror. It was as big as the door and framed in an ornately carved wooden frame. Staring back at me from its surface was not my reflection, but a man I had never met. "Father, this is Michael, the King of this kingdom. Michael this is my father." Rhiannon did quick introductions.

"Hello sir. Rhiannon said you may know what this illness is?" I asked getting straight to the point.

"Yes Your Majesty. I have been on this earth for more than three centuries. I have seen just about every kind of illness that your kind can contract. From what Rhiannon has told me, the illness currently plaguing your people, sounds like one that affected the kingdom 200 years ago. Before we could find a cure, it had wiped out half of the population. Your King and Queen and the Priestesses of the time worked with me and my people. It took us a while, but we eventually found a cure. There is a flower that grew at the top of the mountains. When you boil the petals, it creates a tonic that cures the infected of all traces of the illness. It also makes the uninfected immune to the illness. After discovering this flower, my people started growing it in large amounts around our camps, in case it was needed again. I have already sent some of my people to start making the tonic. Once it is ready, we will start giving it out to the people in the outlands and I will send some to you. By morning, your entire kingdom will be cured and immune." Rhiannon's father explained very quickly.

"Thank you sir! If this works, we will be indebted to you." I said excitedly.

"It is no problem Your Majesty. We may be different, but we are neighbors. My people have always been friendly with yours. My history with your mother in law was a mistake that would not have happened if I had known who she was, but then again I think it was meant to be. For without that mistake, we would not have Rhiannon." He said with a smile.

"Once we have taken care of this illness, we will be having

Rhiannon's birthday ball. I think you should be there sir." I said.

"I would love to attend. Just have Rhiannon let me know the details."

After my conversation with Rhiannon's father, I ran to my chambers. I had to tell Stasia. I came around the corner and instantly knew something was wrong. Samuel was not outside the door, and I could hear Stasia screaming from inside the room. I pushed open the door and was shocked at what I saw.

We had been sitting in my room talking about Lysandra's wedding to keep us distracted from our fears of what was going on outside the room. We had gone through three bottles of wine when all of a sudden, the baby decided it was time she made her entrance into the world. A contraction hit me out of nowhere and I dropped my wine glass. Lina and Lysa jumped up to see what was wrong.

"The baby is coming." I managed to say through the pain. Lina gasped and Lysa turned to Damyen.

"Tell Samuel to find Michael and to get some cloths and warm water." She ordered him. He nodded and ran to the door. Before I knew what was going on, another contraction hit me and I screamed. Lina held my hand as she and Lysa helped me to the bed. Once I was lying down, the contractions started coming quicker and more painfully. All I could do was lie there and scream. I could barely breath, despite Lysa's constant reminders to breath. I could see Damyen sitting back looking very uncomfortable.

All of a sudden, the door burst open and Michael ran in. He froze in the doorway, not expecting to see me lying in bed in full labor. The baby was not due for a few more days. Once the shock had passed he ran over to me. He kissed my forehead and took hold of the hand that Lina was not holding.

"When did it start?" He asked Lysa.

"Just a few minutes ago. We sent Samuel to find you and to bring some cloths and warm water." She answered him quickly.

"Damyen, go find Samuel and help him bring the cloths and water and have somebody find Rhiannon." Michael said. Damyen was relieved to be able to leave.

Once Damyen was gone, Lysandra looked at me and said

"Stasia I am going to see how far you are. It will give us an idea of how long til the baby is here." All I could do was nod. I was in more pain than I expected. I was pretty sure Lina had lost all feeling in her hand and Michael was probably close to it. A moment later, Lysandra looked up at me.

"It should not be much longer before she starts coming. Just try to breath and when you feel her start moving down, make sure you push with each contraction." She coached me.

"You can do this Love. Just breath and before you know it,

you will be holding our little girl in your arms." Michael said before kissing me.

A few minutes later, Damyen walked in with Samuel and Rhiannon right behind him. Rhiannon ran up to me. She knelt down beside Catalina. Damyen and Samuel put the cloth and warm water down next to Lysandra. She turned away from me to speak to them.

"Samuel can you please have the chefs prepare some of Anastasia's favorite tea and some strawberry and crème truffles?" She asked.

"Of course." He said before heading back out.

"Damyen can you go tell the rest of the staff that the heiress will be here within the next few hours. Once you have done that, go rest in your room. You look like you are going to be sick if you stay here much longer." Lysandra said to Damyen who blushed before nodding and heading out.

The next hour or so was the longest hour of my life. It felt as if I was in one long contraction the whole time. Michael and Lina kept trying to comfort me but there was nothing they could really do. Everyone knew that childbirth was immensely painful.

"Is there anything we can do to make it any less painful for her?" Michael asked Lysa.

"No. We have not discovered anything that can ease the pain of childbirth." She said sadly.

"I have seen multiple women give birth, and none of them

have been in this much pain." Lina said confused.

"Wait. I may be able to help." Rhiannon said, surprising everyone.

"What do you mean?" Lysa asked her.

"Stasia told me that the Goddess had said the baby would have power that you have not seen in centuries and her birth would awaken an ancient power in both Stasia and Michael. That means I may be able to use some of my powers to ease her birth. When one of my kind gives birth the women cast a sort of spell over the mother to help bring the baby into the world. The spell can make childbirth worse for your kind, but it should work for Stasia because the baby is not a normal human." Rhiannon explained.

"I do not like the idea. Stasia is in enough pain. What if it does not work and it makes it worse?" Catalina said worried. Michael looked at me. He could see the pain in my eyes. He looked back up to Rhiannon.

"Do it." He said. She nodded and climbed on to the bed. She picked up my head and sat down with my head in her lap. She placed her hands on either side of my head and closed her eyes. She started chanting softly in a language none of us had ever heard before. After a few minutes, the pain started lessening. The contractions still hurt but I no loner felt like I was being torn apart. I looked at Michael with a soft smile on my face.

"It is working." He said with a grin. Rhiannon kept the spell going.

About an hour after Rhiannon started the spell, the baby started coming. It took only about thirty minutes before she was out. Lysandra cleaned her up before wrapping her in a small blanket and handing her to me. Rhiannon had moved back to Lina's side and Michael was sitting next to me. We stared down at our daughter in silence. The only noise in the room was the sounds of Lysandra cleaning up. I kissed my daughter's forehead before turning to Michael.

"Adelaide" was all I said and he smiled before looking back at the baby. He stroked her cheek.

"It is perfect. Princess Adelaide." He said. Catalina squealed. She had been waiting months to find out what the baby's name would be. I had not even told her what we were considering. I kissed the baby before letting my sisters take turns holding their niece.

A knock on the door made all of us jump. Lysandra answered it.

"I am sorry to interrupt but Princess Rhiannon's father is here." Samuel said as he looked over to us. He smiled at the baby before looking to Michael.

"Thank you, Samuel. Please have him wait in the throne room." Michael said. Samuel nodded and left.

"Why is Rhiannon's father here?" I asked.

"That is what I was coming to tell you when I walked in and found you in labor. Her father has a cure for the illness. He said he would hand it out to everyone in the outlands and then have some sent here. I did not expect him to deliver it himself." Michael informed me.

"My father is a man of surprises." Rhiannon said with a smile.

"Okay well I am coming too." I said as I started sitting up.

"You should rest Stasia." Lysandra said worriedly.

"I am fine. Whatever that spell was, it did not just help the pain during, but I am also in no pain now. I do not want to sit in this room any longer." I said sounding more like a queen, than a woman who just gave birth. Michael helped me up and Lysa got me dressed. Catalina followed us to the throne room, holding the baby.

A man was pacing in front of the thrones when we entered. Upon our entrance he froze.

"I am sorry for the surprise visit, but I had been trying to contact Rhiannon for hours with no response. I got worried and decided to come check on things to make sure the illness had not gotten here before I did." He apologized.

"It is alright sir. After our conversation earlier, I went to tell my wife what was going on, and I walked in to her in labor. Rhiannon was aiding her sister through the birth." Michael explained.

"Oh my! That is not what I expected to find, but it is much better! Congratulations!" He exclaimed.

"Father let me introduce you to my sisters. This is Princess Catalina and Queen Anastasia." Rhiannon said proudly.

"It is nice to meet you Your Highness, Your Majesty." He said with a slight bow.

"It is nice to meet you as well." I said as I sat down on my throne, "Michael said you had a cure?"

"Yes, I do. My men are bringing it in now. It is a tonic made from the petals of a special flower that used to only grow at the top of the mountains, but after the last outbreak of this illness, my people have been growing it in case it was needed again. I have had it distributed to the outlands, and it is starting to be distributed to the rest of the kingdom. Those infected in the outlands have been brought back to full health since drinking the tonic. I just wish I had been able to get it out before so many died." He informed with a sad smile.

"Do we have an idea of how many lives it has taken?" I asked curiously.

"My men at last count reported almost 100 deaths." Rhiannon's father reported sadly.

Before I could respond, Samuel walked in with a couple men I had never met. They were each carrying a barrel.

"Ah finally. Your Majesty, this is the tonic. You drink a cup of this and you will be immune to the illness. I believe I have enough here for your family and your entire staff, but if not I can have more brought." Rhiannon's father said sounding happier.

"Thank you sir." I said as I sent Lysandra to get cups.

"Please, call me Adam, Your Majesty." He said with a smile. Lysandra returned with cups and Adam's men poured each of us a cup of the tonic.

"What about the baby?" Damyen said after we had all drank ours.

"I do not think the baby needs it." Rhiannon said.

"Why not?" He asked confused.

"Because if the spell I did during her birth worked, that means she is not human." Rhiannon explained.

"May I look at her?" Adam asked me. I nodded and he stepped up in front of my throne. He knelt down and looked at the baby in my arms. He placed his hand over her heart for a moment.

"Rhiannon is right." He said looking at me.

"Then what is she?" I asked.

"I do not know. I have only ever seen humans and my kind. She is neither." He told me before turning to Rhiannon, "What made you try the spell?" He asked her.

"Stasia told me that the Goddess told them that their daughter would be born with a power that had not been seen in centuries and her birth would awaken an ancient power in Stasia and Michael." Rhiannon told her father.

"Your Majesty, can you give the baby to your sister for a moment?" Adam asked me.

"Sure but why?" I asked as I handed Catalina the baby. "I want to see if I can sense the power in you and your husband, but if you are holding the baby, her power would block yours." He explained.

"That makes sense." Michael said stepping up beside me.

Adam took both of our hands and closed his eyes. He

started chanting. While his chant built in intensity, I could feel a heat spreading from his hand through my body. A sudden intake of breath next to me told me Michael could feel it too. A moment later, Adam let go of our hands and looked up at us.

"Whatever this power is, it is from before my time. I can sense it in both of you, but I have never felt anything like it before. My guess is it will awaken fully overnight. When you two wake up tomorrow, you will have gone through some sort of change." Adam said sounding breathless.

"What do you mean change?" Rhiannon asked.

"I think it will be like when our kind shut down so our bodies can adjust to our power." He told her.

Michael and I headed back to our room a little while later. I had left Catalina in charge of making sure everyone in the palace received some of the tonic. Rhiannon brought Adam to a guest room. Everything seemed to be solved with our people, so now all Michael and I had to deal with was being new parents to our beautiful baby girl, who was sleeping in her father's arms at that moment and trying to figure out what was going on with us. We had no clue what this ancient power was that would be awakening within us over night, and if Adam who had been on this earth for over three centuries had never seen anything like it, was there even a record of it? I was scared to find out what it was but I tried not letting Michael see my fear.

Michael laid Adelaide in her crib, before joining me in our bed. He pulled me into his arms and kissed me.

"I love you Ana!" he whispered.

"I love you too Michael!" I said before snuggling into his chest.

"It is okay to be scared my love. I am too." He said softly.

"You were not supposed to catch that." I said looking up at him.

"Come on Ana. We have been together for eight years. I can read you like a book. You cannot keep stuff like that from me."

"You are right. I am just so used to having to be strong for my sisters and for the kingdom."

"No one is around. It is just us, so relax. Everything will be okay, and remember you are not doing this alone. Whatever this power is, it is awakening in both of us. We will go through it together." Michael said as he kissed me. I kissed him back before falling asleep.

That night my head was full of strange dreams. It seemed like my subconscious was remembering all the monster movies I had watched in the other realm. In one of the dreams, the power inside Michael and I turned us into mer-people. Another turned us into werewolves. The last one I remembered had us as creatures who could change shape at will.

Chapter Eight

I woke up the next morning to an aching pain in my shoulders and a face full of feathers. I opened my eyes and saw that the feathers were actually wings and they were coming out of Michael's back. I screamed. Michael jumped as my scream woke him up. He turned his head and saw the wings and screamed himself. The pain in my shoulders got stronger and it felt like the skin over my shoulder blades was tearing. I screamed in pain as a set of wings burst out of my own back.

Samuel came running in at the sound of our screams. The sight in front of him made him freeze in the doorway.

"Samuel go get my sisters." I said quietly but he heard me. He nodded and backed out of the room.

Michael and I sat there staring at each other in silence for a moment. Finally, he reached out as if he were going to touch my wings but moved very slowly. I could tell we were both thinking the same thing, *These cant be real.* When his hand finally made contact with my feathers, we both gasped. It seemed there were nerve endings in each of the feathers. His touch sent a wave of shock through my entire body.

Before we had a chance to say anything, Catalina came running in. Damyen was right behind her. They both froze in the doorway just like Samuel had. Lina gasped and ran over to me. She sat on the edge of the bed next to me and just stared at our wings. Damyen walked over slowly.

"Stasia?" Catalina asked as if she was hoping it was not actually me.

"Yes." was all I could say. She reached out and stroked one of my wings.

"They are so soft." She said in awe.

We were interrupted by a knock at the door.

"Come in." Michael called. It was Rhiannon. She walked in and was shocked by the sight in front of her but it did not halt her like everyone else. I guess she has seen a lot of strange things growing up as a mystical being.

"How?" She asked.

"We do not know. I woke up a little while ago because I felt a pain in my shoulders and felt feathers in my face. I opened my eyes to see his wings, and a moment later mine tore their way out of my back." I answered her. It felt strange talking about Michael and I having wings.

"I have heard stories from my people of an ancient race that sported wings like an angel, but they were before us. Damyen can you get my father? I think he was heading to the banquet hall." Rhiannon said.

"Of course." Damyen said before heading out.

Lysandra walked in all of a sudden.

"Stasia, breakfast is.." She started to say but cut herself off when she saw the scene in front of her.

"Oh goddess!" She exclaimed.

"Lysa, can you take Adelaide to the nursery and feed her for me? I will come get her when we are done talking to Adam." I asked, noticing that the baby was waking up. How she slept through Michael and I screaming on her first morning out of the womb, I will never know.

"Of course Stasia." Lysa answered as she walked over and picked up my daughter.

Once they were gone we went back to silence. No one had any idea what to say. Michael decided to break the silence by spreading his wings out. They were huge. He flapped them a couple of times and they created a strong breeze in our bedroom. Mine and the girls' hair was going crazy. I decided to join him and see how it felt. I stretched them out and tried flapping them a few times. It definitely felt weird, to say the least.

Damyen came back with Adam while we were playing with our wings. Damyen walked over and stood by Catalina as Adam walked right up to me. The look on his face was one of pure amazement and awe. "I cannot believe it." He said softly. "What?" Michael asked a little impatient.

"My kind tell stories of the ancient winged beings. Everyone thinks they are just creatures of legend, but I know differently. When I was young, before I had even accessed my magic, I came upon a cave. Inside the cave was the body of a woman with large angelic wings. None of my people before me had even known about them. My parents sent me to try and find out what they were. My search took me to the lands on the other side of the mountains. These lands are filled with all kinds of mystical creatures, but it is ruled by a community of Wise Women, as my people call them. These women are the daughters of the Gods. They know of all the mystical creatures of the past and the present. They can tell you everything you need to know about your new powers." Adam said, the look of awe still on his face.

After the conversation with Adam, I sent Catalina and Rhiannon to get things ready for Rhiannon's birthday ball, and sent Damyen to send word to the temple of what has happened recently, including mine and Michael's transformations. Michael went to talk to the guards and I went to the nursery. Everyone that Michael or I passed in the halls stopped to stare. You would think with my position in society since birth that I would be used to being the center of attention, but I was not. It felt so good to finally get to the nursery.

Adelaide was lying on the floor in the middle of the play area. Lysandra was seated next to her showing her some of the little toys. It seemed Adelaide's favorite was a little stuffed bird. She kept reaching for the wings and giggling. I stood near the door and just watched my daughter for a few moments. It was calming, after everything I had gone through lately and everything I was dealing with. She broke me out of my trance a moment later. She turned her little head and smiled right at me. After that I could not just stand back and watch. I dropped down next to her and started playing too. For a baby only a day old, she moved quite a bit.

Lysandra and I sat in the nursery playing with Adelaide for a few hours before Michael came in to find me. He picked up the baby and told me to follow him., so I did. He led me down to my dressing chambers. Shealah was inside with a rack of new gowns and a basket of baby clothes.

"Ana!" She cried when she saw me.

"Shea, what are you doing here? I thought you would be getting ready for your wedding." I asked confused.

"Michael sent word to me about what happened this morning, and I figured you could use some new clothes that would accommodate the wings. I went through my stock and brought you every low back gown I had in your size. I also found some beautiful baby dresses I just had to bring for the little princess." Shea said with a smile.

"Oh thank you Shea. Do you have something I can wear to Rhiannon's ball tonight?" I asked excitedly. I always loved new clothes.

"Of course. I even have something for Adelaide."

Shea and I spent the next hour trying on dresses. I finally settled on a purple off the shoulder gown. It was silk and the back was just low enough to be comfortable underneath my wings. There was even a baby version of the gown for Adelaide.

After we got dressed, Adelaide and I went to find the others. Catalina was in the ballroom overseeing the last of the decorating. When I walked in everyone froze. Catalina stared at me for a moment before recovering. She walked up to me and pulled me aside.

"What was that about? By now everyone has seen our wings." I asked Lina quietly.

"That was not just for the wings. You looked like a completely different person for a moment. There was an ethereal aura around you. It was strange and beautiful at the same time." She explained to me.

"Okay I cannot take any more of these surprises. Tomorrow, Michael and I are going to the other side of the mountains to find out as much as we can. I will leave you in charge until we return." I said a little exasperated.

Michael walked in then just in time, but he was not alone. Lady Demetrya was with him. She bowed to me and smiled at Adelaide who was lying in my arms giggling.

"Lady Demetrya, how nice to see you." I said politely.

"Thank you Your Majesty. When we received word from your brother in law about what had happened I had to come down." She said with a smile.

"Thank you. It is a big surprise, but so far all we know is that we have wings. I decided that tomorrow we will travel to the lands beyond the mountains and meet with the Wise Women over there. Adam said that they will be able to help us." I informed her and Michael.

"Who is Adam? How does he know about the Wise Women?" Lady Demetrya asked confused. "Adam is my sister Rhiannon's father who we just met yesterday. He is the leader of the mystical beings that live at the base of the mountains. As a child he stumbled upon the body of a woman with wings like ours and his parents sent him to find out what she was. His search brought him to the Wise Women." I explained and then added, "He is also the one who cured the kingdom of that illness that was killing everyone the last few days."

"I was not aware his people were still in the mountains." She said matter of factly but her expression looked like she was hiding something. Before I cold question her on it, Damyen walked in.

"Stasia, Rhiannon needs your help with her ball gown." He said, sounding very bored. I nodded before handing Adelaide to Michael and heading down to Rhiannon's dressing chambers.

Rhiannon was inside with Shealah. They were arguing over some part of the gown that Rhiannon was wearing. I stood in the doorway and laughed. It was just like the conversation I had with Shealah before my last birthday ball (before my disappearance). My laughter halted their argument.

"What is so funny Stasia?" Rhiannon asked slightly angry.

"Oh nothing. It is just that I had that same exact argument with Shealah before my fourteenth birthday ball." I said still chuckling.

"I remember. Your mother stormed in wondering what was taking so long and she started laughing at us." Shealah said with a smile.

The Ball went smoothly. There were no tragedies and no crimes committed. We had finally had a successful event, the first since my disappearance three years earlier. Rhiannon danced the night away with her new fiance, and Catalina managed to keep everyone from asking questions about me and Michael. By the time midnight came I was ready for a long sleep.

The next morning Lysandra woke us up early. She already had us all packed for our journey, even the baby's stuff. Michael and I got dressed quickly while Lysa dressed the baby for me. After a quick breakfast, we said goodbye to my sisters and headed out with Adam. He would bring us through the mountains.

The journey was long but quite beautiful. It had been years since I had traveled through my kingdom. I loved seeing all the people out and about. They all stopped to wave at us. The lands beyond the villages were even more beautiful. Wild flowers grew everywhere, and the wild life was countless. A few hours later, we had finally gotten to the foot of the mountains, where we stopped to take a break to eat. This was where Adam's people lived.

The community Adam and his people built here was beautiful. Everyone worked together to keep it going. There was no separation by rank or power. Adam was their leader, but he still got his hands dirty with the menial everyday work. Watching them for the short while Michael and I were among them, made me desire a community like that in my kingdom.

During the rest of the journey through the mountains, I told Michael of my new desires for our kingdom. He loved the idea, but he was doubtful it would work with our people. Our kingdom has lived the same way for centuries and the people were not ones for change. We spent the duration of the journey discussing possible futures for our family and our kingdom.

It was just about sunrise when we finally made it out of the mountains. Adam gave us directions to the little village of the Wise Women and left us to return to his people. Michael and I decided to use our wings to make the journey a bit quicker. Michael carried our bags while I carried Adelaide. We flew for a little over an hour before coming to the gates that led to the village. Adam said these gates were spelled to not let any through unless their intentions were pure. We landed in front of them and walked slowly through. As we passed through the gates, we could feel the power rush through us. Even Adelaide felt it, as she giggled in my arms. A short ways down a footpath and we came to the village, where we were met by a beautiful young woman who made me instantly jealous of her beauty.

She greeted us as Lady Davina and welcomed us to the village. Then she led us into a small cottage where he offered us tea and biscuits.

"Your Goddess told me you would be coming to us. I could not believe at first that she had awakened more of your kind after so long, but she was always unpredictable." Lady Davina said with a smile as we sipped our tea.

"What is our kind?" I asked getting straight to the point.

"Myself and the other women of this village are called the daughters of the Gods. That is not true. We are the daughters of one goddess and a human man. Your kind are called Descendants because you are descended directly from the Gods. The first of your kind were born of two divine parents. Every generation after got a little less of the divine power and eventually your kind died out. But it was said that one of the goddesses who mothered the firsts would be able to awaken more Descendants and they would be as pure as if she had birthed them herself." She explained.

"So you are saying that we are pretty much the children of the Goddess in literal terms?" I questioned.

"Basically yes."

"So what does it mean to be a Descendant? What are our abilities and such?" Michael jumped in.

"Well first off is the obvious, the wings. You can also wield magic as we can. You can manipulate the elements, and you cannot die until you have achieved a status of divinity so that upon your deaths you may be welcomed into the home of the Gods as only their children can be." Lady Davina answered Michael's question as if she were reading items off a shopping list.

After our first conversation with Lady Davina, she introduced us to her sisters. They all helped us in one way or another to learn about our new abilities and how to use them. Three days after we had arrived in the village, I was reading through a spell book and came across a spell that would fix a problem my family thought unfixable. The spell would make it so a woman who was born without the ability to bare children would be able to bare but one child. After Lady Davina assured me that the spell truly does work, I packed us up and Michael and I flew home.

I wanted to share with Catalina that I had found a way to make her dreams come true. Though when I arrived home I found a scene I was not prepared for. Lysandra met us in the entryway.

"Stasia, Michael, I have some amazing news." She said sounding both excited and confused.

"What is it Lysa?" I demanded.

"Catalina is with child."

The End

Made in the USA
Middletown, DE
10 September 2023

38156004R00070